W9-BSN-995

An Island Death

By the same author

AN ISLAND DEATH
SOMEONE JUST LIKE YOU
VOICES OF BROOKLYN (EDITOR)
THE BAG
FERTIG
THE WARRIORS

HARPER & ROW, PUBLISHERS
NEW YORK · EVANSTON · SAN FRANCISCO · LONDON

An Island

SOL YURICK

Death

 For information address Harper & Row, Publishers, Inc., 10 East 53rd Street, New York, N.Y. 10022. Published simultaneously in Canada by Fitzhenry & Whiteside Limited, Toronto.

FIRST EDITION

Designed by Gloria Adelson

Library of Congress Cataloging in Publication Data

Yurick, Sol, 1925–
An island death.
I. Title.
PZ4.Y95Is [PS3575.U7] 813'.5'4 74–15898
ISBN 0–06–014784–9

71 72 73 74 75 10 9 8 7 6 5 4 3 2 1

For Susanna
You used to ask me
why I never left for work
like other fathers.
This is why.

1

The first thing Helen did was to walk swiftly across the room and put her strong arm, her tennis arm, around Targ's shoulder and squeeze fiercely and guide his head to between her breasts. "It's all right. It's all right," she whispered.

How swift to see she was. "Who are you?"

She ignored the question. He shouldn't have asked. Our marriage was coming apart. Therefore that was who she was.

"You're shivering, darling. Come upstairs. Do you have a fever?"

No, Targ thought; I'm going crazy. Never had she, one of them, the as-wife, been more magnificent, never fiercer. The best yet. How they knew what he longed for. And all the ingrained harsher lines hatred had engraved on her face swiftly mutated to lines of pity at his terror. This was the most important part; how smoothly she would do it. Her arm held tighter and tighter. Targ wouldn't have thought her, a woman, so strong. And when he thought "her" so familiarly, it restored, in fact, family. He accepted; she accepted; it became easier; her forcefulness relaxed. He should have known: the she was built for better things. He began to fill in. She had brought him this far; she was determined to bring him all the way up. He stood shivering in the warm living-room air. Someone had turned the titled spines of the ten-thousand *absolutely-necessary,* the for-survival books, wallward. He followed her distracted eyes scanning; waited for her to comment. She said nothing. Good touch. And the love, the *love*—now that he needed her, now that she could pilot him once more—radiated from her. She, holding him, protecting him, was having something like an orgasm. He was grateful. He was resentful. Should he put his hand between her legs to test? No. But his hand slid up. Reflex. She didn't recoil. They *were* married.

"It's curious, but I'm hungry, terribly hungry," he told her.

"What do you want?"

"Anything. Give me a piece of bread."

They went into the kitchen. His knees were trembling. He sat down at the table.

"I'll fix you something. Some pancakes, Targ—"

"No!" he yelled. "Just give me a piece of bread. Basics . . ."

She gave him a slice of bread, soft white bread, but his hands were trembling so that he had to prop his elbows on the table and press down hard, and squirreled his food in, stuffing his cheeks. "Just a moment of panic," he dribbled.

Soft white bread. No, not basics. There were no basics anymore. He tore pieces and squeezed, mixing her vagina moisture and bread into a magic glue, shaping a breast-studded torso, and bit. He used to do that when he was a kid. He made a discovery; the squashed bread shapes were like those Stone-Age "Venuses." He bit more selectively this time. His agitation increased. He radiated it. She ingested his madness and grew fuller. He tasted blood and metal. Chemicals? Bloody gums? Put his finger there. White matter: masticated bread and saliva. No blood; whose blood? What had his mother called it? *Kvatch.* Unhealthy.

"Do you want toast?"

"No, too abrasive."

This is my body; eat. Jesus Christ, was he *that* bad off? Couldn't he face his own dissolution without giving it a lifeless allusion? And yet it comforted him because it told him what was happening to him. Guideline words.

"Just stick out the year, Targ," she said.

For a second he didn't recognize what he was being called. Answered to Trag. No. Had changed his name a long time ago to Targ. Learned to live with it. Stick it out? It would kill him. She just didn't understand.

"No, I understand. Stick it out. We'll stand by you. Don't I always?" She held his wrist and squeezed him still harder with the other hand. "Didn't I always, Targ?"

She was right. She kept him from giving way and for that he . . . hated her. Had for a long time. "I can't bear it," he said. He was also very drunk.

"Try," she cajoled, and stroked his head. Her hand left a burning, acid trace across the transparent skin of his forehead.

"If I go wild, you'll be responsible." Then he shouted: wordless, or rather whole speeches intensely compressed and scrambled into a half-second. A burst, standing for "We are all dying and I can no longer bear their rutting bodies, the blank, insipid, grass-blowing, gum-chewing faces, the stubborn, blank, impregnable faces they present to me every day, faces as bland as their Polaroid identification portraits . . . and . . ." "And yet, *we* did that to them, didn't we?" and looked directly at Helen for the first time. Her face was blank. Tactic: agree with the madman. Not knowing yet what Targ might have done, she waited. Had he done something irrevocable and thus blocked himself forever in the climb to the heights? Was the chancellor-to-be Targ, head of the growing New University in the womb of the Old University, which interfaced commerce to cosmos, across continents, to remain forever merely Professor Targ, a once-bright-young-man grown old and futile? Unable to make the transition? Old departments would atrophy. Offices would be boarded up, mason's nails driven through wood and cinderblock, only to be re-opened in the future when they rediscovered Our Ancient Heritage, which would then be retitled The Stages of Evolution Program. He couldn't help worrying he would lose her now, and hated himself for worrying so quickly. How abject. Poor bargaining.

She waited. He would tell it his own way.

Earlier that day he had stood in front of his class, teaching those barbaric hundreds Our Classical Heritage. They came, as usual, in restless, roving bands of two or three hundreds, hungry, empty, anxious, to fill the amphitheater and suck, suck. They left, satiated, needing to devour their three times their weight in facts every day so they could, at examination time, at void-time, shit out the no more than merely required knowledge. The residue was supposed to be their increment of growth. (He thought this at her. He didn't bother saying it out loud. An old discussion between them. An old contention which his frown announced was beginning. Her look of reasonableness, of exquisite and tortured patience, replied to him. They argued above, below, around, behind aural thresholds; savagely, telepathically.) They seemed to listen, engineers, business-administration majors, those premedical morons, law people, the academics and culture soppers, the preanthropologists and even, frequently, the wisdom-of-the-Easters, as well as the Black and Women's studies people who by their expressions of contempt said White Man/Male-Oriented studies . . . listening to the Pageant of the Past, taking their required culture-mead. They were, the joke went, esoteric boxes and the task of the education was to link them into different levels of strings and networks. Now, if one was a good professor, somewhat applause-happy, one gave them witty touches of gossip about The

Great, mentioned the Football season as topical to the sports-mad Spartans, and showed them that a grounding in classics-influenced English permitted, even enhanced, a dry, telling, funny delivery. His style was to speak of himself speaking: "Targ says . . ." Third person.

Actually it was two courses in one. The first course was overt, being merely what it seemed to be. The second was a secret course, coded, understandable to about ten students in three hundred. The cue was to say ". . . s'Targ." ". . ." was a mumbled sound. Indistinct. Genitive. Possessed case. They who succeeded in breaking the coding showed they were fit to listen to what was really said. After they had proved themselves, they would get minute earpieces and listen to other lecturers, who broadcast simultaneously. He too wore an earpiece and heard his own clear voice among the many thousands, his voice heard lagging a fraction of a second behind his spoken words.

As always he scanned them for a sign of, first, puzzlement and then enlightenment, for a facial sign of inner election and ultimate worth, and, third, a furious scribbling, a kind of radiant and active triumph which allowed those few to look around at their fellows victoriously. He had seen couplings break up their romances in the middle of a lecture. It was how his own marriage had begun to break up. The next test would be to see how long they could sustain their discovery that things were not what they seemed.

While discussing the rape of Rome by the Barbaric Hordes, and the measures taken, the social antibodies generated to encapsulate the infection, convert it by culture, and then to assimilate it, Targ watched (detached from the taste of *that* flesh by about fourteen hundred years) a pantiless little girl, her plump knees, her casually mocking thighs held apart, as she leaned over to her neighbor and looked at his notebook and let him smell her young sex. It was spring. The sexual dissonance, the noise of it, was deafening. Class would soon be over, but mate hunting or rutting, never. They would walk, bumping against one another, over the sweet lawn, or through the hallowed halls, then fuck too expertly later, in the dark niches behind the mathematics buildings or in the bushes fringing the manor house lawns. To the *Kamasutra* and *The Perfumed Garden, Screw,* and catalogs of sexual acrobatics on Indian lingams they added the exciting kick of being watched. He had seen them all in the dark corners, under the staircases, in the locker rooms, in the cubicles of the psychology testing labs, in the library stacks, loving, loving. His trouble was that he hadn't succeeded yet in incorporating this sexual dissonance into his approaches to Civilization.

Targ thought, a wild and sudden urge taking him back to "now" from "antiquity," that if he got into that young girl's esoteric box, she would pay attention to what she should be writing down—Slavic verbs, notes on the Persic Empire, Chinese tone ranges, machine translation, carbon dating, structural rules for constructing evolutionary evidence, dismissed, sunken, decayed, Stalinist irrigation empires—for her soft thighflesh up to the not quite virginal vagina was unstained (except for the usual matters of micturition, fingerprints, defecation, and other, female exudations) by the Man's phallic flesh. But this was forbidden since she had shown no particular signs of election.

Targ had turned and written "East/Goths vs. West/Civilization" on the blackboard to hide his unhistoric manhood distorting the warp of time, the woof of empire, the pants fabric of his fly. Helen's legs were much better than those white, immature babyfat childlegs. "Remember this," Targ told them. "It may come up on a testing." "These are better, much better than . . ." Targ told Helen and squeezed the back of her thigh where it joined her behind, which swelled out like the bulb top of an Egyptian lotus column. Since they hadn't had sex for . . . He looked at her. "?" She shrugged. All right, at least two years. So she was surprised and knew he had really gone mad.

Among the voices in his earpiece he heard his own voice saying, ". . . Trag's view of this event is . . ." Then Targ felt the floor tremble as though an earthquake had taken place. He listened for the slip again. **Among the intense, compressed learning mes-**

sages he heard new sounds: groans, whimpers, moans, pleas, beggings, cries for food, in batches of compressed sound. And then silences as those units of screamers stopped being. He felt an iciness in spite of the languid spring air . . . as if the sun's radiance had been drained away for a second. Something had happened. Did the perpetual fluorescents flicker, go out almost, and adjust to a slightly higher level of energy? The intensity of the flow of knowledge seemed to increase in his ears. The elect seemed to take it in stride: no writhing or blinking. What had taken him years to accept they adjusted to in a second. Was that it? Or something else. Escalation? Was it him or outside him? The shock jumbled all the knowledge in his head, tumbled it, or half decayed it into nothing more or less than an assemblage of mere facts, worse than facts, bits distemporalized, unalphabetized, unstructured, many of which he could recall, but in relation to nothing at all, not even to themselves, not even in the proper sequences. He *heard,* but nothing made sense.

He expected them to look up and notice that he, or the floor, one of them, was trembling terribly. They've started it: some idiot has pressed that button, Targ thought. He tried to comfort himself with litanies of megadeaths and the consolations of Noah Kahn. It didn't work. Accreted smugness did not console for no-future. He heard his own voice alone, in the earpiece, yammering the most outrageous nonsense although the voice that came out of his mouth seemed still to be reasonable and measured. He moaned, looking out the gothic window, seeing the faceless gleaming sheen of the new windowless Barth Building, in which were housed the computers, memory banks, lists of desires sequentially arranged in ascending passion from anxiety to lust/hatred to the wrath of Achilles to International Insensate Spasm. And he had forgotten Greek conjugations, but remembered the crumbling and precious peristyle of some exhumed though now forgotten piece of masonry that was probably no more than some outhouse precious to Ionian conquerors: that much. He forgot the simplest Latin declension and spent three minutes trying to even remember the Latin for the word, the concept "of our love" (it would steady him), and looked out the window passage, again expecting to see Dionysian capers crisped on the microwaved sod. There was nothing more than death-agonizing epileptic twittering student bodies assembled, statued as though dead, in laborious and compulsive copulation, as memorable as flies, midges, all not knowing that they were, as of now, quite extinct.

No, Targ thought. It isn't as much that. But that feeling he was going mad. Agitation and calm. His disturbance wasn't even his own; nevertheless, he felt it acutely. Words failed to shape his anguish, which is to say that what he felt he could not feel intensely without the proper words. And since he couldn't get rid of the words, which formed in his mind, which his tongue and throat insisted on babbling, his disturbance was intensified by each utterance. The song of domestic birds, the feel of spring as a skin irritant, the sounds of pens balling dutifully across the soon-to-be-thrown-away notebook pages; a cough, a fart, a belch, a giggle, a whisper, a voiced and aspirated yawn—these half saved him for a while. "The world's dying," Targ whispered, but said it in Linear B. Two or three of the chosen/self-chosen, the ones he had brought out, caught between the Scylla of expediency and the lure of scholarship, looked up in approbation, smiled on cue, pretending they were in on some special joke. He was once like that. It was how he had got where he was now. Louts. Even the best and the brightest; all. And he culled all the jumbled facts and tried to remember, but didn't have the art and logic to do it.

Outside, the spring madness, the memorial ritual, was taking hold of them all. Ten years were compressed into an afternoon. Febriles danced up and down the sweeping lawns in and around the fucking bodies. Sanes and moderates against the Ultras. Signs were carried and crowns were cracked. Excursions and Alarums. The Liberation factions, their costumes, jargons, and specializations proliferated as they poured out of buildings and into other buildings, seizing them then yielding them up. The air was heavily electronic with rock music and they sang "Blowin' in the Wind" and "Eve of Destruction."

While others longed for the dear dead days beyond recall. Measures were taken to stop this total fragmentation. Lines were formed, columns, mobs, which then dissolved and regrouped. Sometimes others were shot and carried off the field of battle. Was it happening or was it a vision? And his head was crashed down into shards.

"But I'm not going to let any head shrinker excavate the ruins of Ancient Targ," Targ told Helen.

"You don't have to. Come upstairs and lie down. Give in to it. Let it take hold of you."

A trap. No Laingian abjectness for him.

"No, you don't have to do that either."

"I hate them. I hate those little snots who want to return to the past. I hate those little snots who want the workable future. I hate their ambition. I hate their apathy."

"I hate them too," she, his ultimate prize and passage ticket, said. She lied. And her bronzed tennis arm squeezed again. Muscles played beneath the tan patina. Sweat and Ban contended for pheromonic dominance, both exciting.

How was he going to reach them? They took him like medicine to make them grow, or an obstacle along the way to technicianhood. The blank-faced and barbaric spawn of the intelligent and democratic middle class looked at Targ with intelligent-faced amiability, feeling nothing, waiting to feel, regarding nothing of the warning he gave them. He became a ghost, though they wouldn't have called it that.

The bell tolled the knell of parting class and they all dispelled, except for the few misplaced earnests who were stirring against the bonds of process, looking for the slightest advantage. They wanted to ask questions: they knew he had the keys. Recognizing what they were doing, of course, he became difficult, cryptic, evasive, talked in aphorisms . . . to test them, of course. And yet he had been like that once, coming out of the working class himself, out of vast six-story apartment houses, gone through the Korean War, gone to the then undreamed-of schools because of the great Amnesty Act

(P.L. 346), searching the mazes to the right professors' teas, learning the first great foreign style-tongues, wearing costumes, shedding savagery like snake skins, metamorphosing in stages, bringing into actual being every child's dream, that he was a changeling and really from some royal family, breaking down their language codes, to be restored to his rightful inheritance. In the old days, Oxford and Cambridge scholars could pass disguised as mad Mahdis and Arab slavers; but could Arab pilgrims pass as Anglo-classical gentlemen? It was a question of reversing the process, laving away layers of the past. And to that purpose he took more speech clinics and acting courses than most. It was a question of Anglo-Saxonizing the self . . . and he had been ruthless to the point of shedding an embarrassing wife. He had even managed to change his name (Trag into Targ) by sneaking around and changing the spelling on every identification document he could get his hands on. The forgeries were clumsy. He knew it; they knew it. That they didn't act had been a signal to him that his ambition, his ruthlessness, his first act of self-negation and rebirth was accepted. He had come home to his wife. He couldn't tell her. He would have to get rid of her. This was the second requirement. He wept.

Targ controlled himself. Anyway, he couldn't have answered a one of the elect at the moment. He said it was over for now, perhaps forever; they laughed dutifully (what else could it be but a joke?), tucked books under their arms, and left.

"Philidor" (with whom Targ was writing a new Universal History of the World, Ancient to Medieval Times, 1000 A.D., commissioned by a publisher who would—they would too—make a small fortune on it; it was to be used as a text and wouldn't be too difficult for preoccupied premedicals, prelaws, and precaptains of industry to understand; and what with a revision every five years, to keep abreast of the times, they would prosper and increase) "is a fag," Trag told Helen.

"I know, sweetheart," she said, but her stony eyes did not accept any Trag but worried only about Targ, loving him more because he was sick, wondering if their ten years together were going to go out the window and would Targ never get to rule the New University? They had no children. That was it. A sacrifice. End of the genetic line.

"Don't worry," Targ told her, "I didn't compromise. We'll have it." And yet he must have done something bad, because here she was.

Because he had gone out of the classroom and walked across the sun-and-oak-stippled lawn, watching the hot insects shimmering and fluttering and mating and spawning in the warm air, smelled the green of crushed grass, the heavy spring perfume of tended flowers, watched other moths in denim shorts or short skirts, crew-cut heads or tossing, shining, shampooed heads, mating too. And he had come to the office he shared with Philidor. They sat, Philidor doing the talking, mostly babbling this or that departmental gossip, who was not sleeping with whom, and how they should handle the decay of the Roman Empire ("It never died," sang he. "Massive lead poisoning . . . the end of biological lines of descent. Deferred technology . . ."

"The secret and abiding bureaucracies, the secret societies," said Philidor, "to say nothing of the New Men. All contending. The Jews taking over and becoming in the process non-Jews, becoming what they changed, killing themselves by rewriting their own history . . ."

"Shouldn't we say that?"

"No. That's not what we're paid to say") and the rise of the Dark Ages.

"The sun shone then," Targ told him.

Philidor laughed. "Dear boy, to be sure."

"Because the darkness was in the minds of those who came before." And he launched into the decay of carbon dating, new theories about the movement of continents, the new demography and the supermodern ancient medicine, and all the other now upset standards. "Shouldn't we begin with the Celtish civilization, at whose end the Dark Ages really begin?"

Philidor got quite upset.

"And you know that would knock his camp agenda right out of the closet," he told Helen.

"Ah, yes. Rapture about the universality of belief . . . the five-or six-hundred-year placebo. I know all that, Targ." Philidor shrugged, thinking about something else, turning his slender, bow-nosed, high-cheeked, blond-capped face toward the window and sighing. "It is a dollar, Targ, dear boy," and ejected a cigarette stump from his ebony holder. "It is our contribution to the preservation of civilization as we know it. I mean where would progress go?"

They were in the eight hundreds and Hrudland—called Roland, or even Orlando—fights in the pass. "But we must include . . ." and Targ told him what.

Philidor looked at Targ, astonished. "But, Targ, that just happened a few days ago."

"I know."

"Dear boy, you're joking."

"Well, isn't the present past? Time present and time past and time future contained in real time?"

"Ah, you've been playing those stupid computer simulations games."

"I mean they've dropped it. Salvo."

"Targ, who dropped what?"

"The bomb. A bomb. It's a matter of moments before the wave reaches us. And we all, everything, become radiant hellfire. Burning particles shimmering in the nothingness. Big-bang theory. Hurried up the Om theory. Unity with the great ground of being. All facts and events equal inside the memory bank. Wisdom of the Orient technologized and numbered."

"Targ, that is as it may be, but I'm not going to argue metaphysics with you."

"Atomizing war is not metaphysics."

"Oh, yes it is, Targ."

"I *know,* I tell you. After all, I'm a historian, a classicist, who has the power of the past and the gift of a few minutes of the future . . . what's left of it."

"I think we ought to put it that Roland and Oliver and Charlemagne stopped the March of Islamic Culture at—"

"And preserved the Dark Ages in order that democracy might rise in its proper sequence."

"Well, you can't make an ommmmelet . . ." Philidor said and made a ritual pass at his balls, grasped air, and squeezed viciously. "Thus I refute *thee. . . .*"

"Listen, Philidor, you alone would know. *Sug mir den emmus . . .*" (Where did that Yiddish phrase come from? What was interfering?) "Did Roland and Oliver belong to a secret society which sucks and fucks each other?"

"As much as you and I do, baby. You know, I've always suspected you of being a closet straight."

Our leaders make peace, yet want to burn bombs like firecrackers to keep the new Islamic hordes the other side of our Roncesvalles, Targ thought. "Because such holocausts antique us one and all, and what are we on but a kind of dramatic archaeological expedition, not even historians, only with more resources than other expeditions ever had: I mean newspapers and simulations games and such, Philidor."

"Dear boy . . ."

"So dig it, Philidor," Targ told him and waved the morning *Times* at him. "Everything's going to be ruined and secularized."

"Oh, for heaven's sake," Philidor said and got up and went out; and that was all the work they did that afternoon.

Targ followed Philidor to an interdepartmental and interdisciplinary tea. The wild clown inside him was surprised that his outside could, for a while, make some sort of urbane chatter to the other faculty lights, to the treasured few students they all groomed as Carriers of the Light (though disease would be a better name for it), admitted to the sanctum sanctorum (as Targ had been groomed and admitted by wise old Professor Biddle). He followed Philidor around the room, clowned a little to make him unhappy, watched cliques form rank, sects bunch up to glare wildly at one another, and come apart; watched secret assignations being made under the cover of talking about That New Chaucer Paper, Dialectical Affinities, or Studies Toward a Prolegomena of the Philosophy of Authenticity; saw them all strive toward one another, seeking contact, or recoil, hating with all their faculties. Powerful old Norn ladies with heavy reputations in anthropology, comparative languages, Germanic and Slavic studies, who had written vital studies for the Rand Corporation, the War College, the CIA, and suchlike, served tea and frittered in brightly colored frocks and straw hats too insubstantial for their massive heads, their voices careening through one or two preciously high octaves while they slid back and forth on their unstroked rumps and parchmenty vaginas. (No, no longer so; since the great reorganization, everyone got serviced.) He hated them too, having had to ascend through and on and under them too. Poet-ambassadors and ambassadresses who had done important work for International Understanding and sopped up the tragico-lyric material that was the stuff of their intense, short-form sufferings floated by.

Something was wrong, however. Some peculiar quirk of arrangement. The wrong people were matched up and didn't stay together long enough. The ritual was perfunctory. Its movements were . . . what? Cacophonic. Or had he, who was so swift to read a scattered-out hierarchy, lost the ability to do so? Usually the luminaries were surrounded by galactic wheelings of acolytes, and between them the unaffiliated and undecided among the attractive clumps, but that didn't seem to be the case today. Were there new luminaries? New centers? Across the room he could see his own followers seeking blindly as if they didn't see him; or did he move too fast?

He bumped into Philidor's arm, trying to make him spill his tea, but Philidor didn't feel him. He was busy assimilating a new young assistant with a thin face, all sensitive bone, dark like an Assyrian courtier's, oh, say two days before that empire was swept into the dust bins of history. The Assyrian had been culled in an Institute for International Education dragnet from Iran, saved from peasant parents and parasites by missionaries who had fed him, fucked him, and delivered him up.

". . . totality and universality of the Mother Church in *le moyen âge . . ."* the acolyte said.

Philidor held the boy's necklace between forefinger and thumb and rhythmically stroked the horn hypnoglyph between his pectorals, saying amorously, ". . . but Albigensians, Waldensians, Cathers, Brunists, Manicheans, Beghards, and Beguines . . . secret societies encamped, ready to truck off at a moment's notice. Heresies spawned, dear boy, simply *spawned* . . . all leading to the age of constipation and sexual constraint brought on by that dreadful and humorless lout Luther, that early disorder known as the Reformation, if you will."

"But there was no possibility of true dissent," the boy's plump lips sighed.

"And to say nothing of the scandals of John the twenty-third, a *pope,* mind you, who was given to . . ." Philidor said to the dark, earnest face, his lips close to the boy's ear.

"But atheism was simply impossible to *think,"* and the boy's voice was feminized and he acquiesced and their cups rattled together. Philidor turned to Targ, winked as if to say: You see, no matter what I say they can't untrack. . . . Targ turned and found his face next to the fleshly shoulders, pouring out of her low dress, of the dean's wife. The skin was quite white, quite unstained by the sun. He reached down and pinched her flesh where it ballooned out a little between the girdle's cut and her stocking's compress. She, an veteran of faculty teas, was grateful to Targ because he didn't have to do that sort of thing anymore, and she laughed quite on time to bald-topped, false-toothed Professor Mithers's joke (he was an ancient man wearing a three-button suit and hair down to his shoulders, who always began his lectures by saying, "Now, you must understand that Milton did not consider Lucifer in the least attractive"). Targ knew the tea was spiked with spirit and he was getting drunker. The smell of grass was in the air. Others took cocaine. It would dissolve into a mass fuck later: the unibeast. And he knew he was truly invisible; he had to leave and see the interim chancellor. He had had enough; he had paid his dues.

But they are wise old men, these chancellors, and sense the coming of a crisis because they see into the grand distances. The chancellor was one of those grand old men. Actually not so old. He was one of old Biddle's boys too, but from an earlier cycle, from before the Second World War. He had gone into the war as an intelligence agent and it had changed him completely. He emerged with a sense of mission and fought tenaciously to preserve and advance civilization against the forces of darkness.

He played, now, the lovable character who talked of the Sweep and Drama of History as if it were a tragic entertainment in Viconian acts, a closet drama for which All Man had been enlisted. But Grand Old Men do not lead transformations to the New University; his special genius was that he knew he couldn't do it alone. And Targ could remember a certain time (somehow he always thought of it as taking place at night) in 1967 when it seemed as if it were all, twenty years of careful buildup, coming apart. There had been a twenty-six-hour conference on how they would contain the rise of those new internal barbarians, the students—in fact, use the barbarians to restructure civilization and its fount, the university. No bumbling then; no wise old saws. It was all strategies and tactics then. All universities (esoteric boxes which were assemblages of esoteric boxes—the departments—which were themselves assemblages of esoteric boxes—the students, all screaming for freedom and autonomy) would be fused. The chancellor had turned to him; listened to him; weighed the options; taken chances. A move to the left would clear out the dead wood; a move to the right would then stabilize the gains. Had another move been made without consulting him?

The chancellor received Targ, shook Targ's hand with his manly grip, sat down, sighed two or three times, snuffled once, tapped his silver-ringed pipe against a cork ball into the ashtray, wiped the sensual curve of his brier against the monumental British tweed he wore winter and summer, and sat as ageless and mystical as any Fate. He harumphed, brushed back his white hair, and stared with a calm and loving possessiveness at the Colonial furniture and wainscoting. Targ smelled varnish and felt the thick rug nap under his feet. Around them, on the walls, former deans, chancellors, presidents, bursars, grand educators were lined; all terrific behind the majestic austerity of varnish, carved frames, and glass, immured in prophetic robes, staring down gravely. In cases, treasures from the ancient world were housed: Tang horses, silk scrolls, marbles . . . loot of the world; signs of civilization: the best of the Zaharoff, Peabody, Lansky, and Macy collections.

But the chancellor *knew.* He sensed. He told Targ that he and he alone was the chancellor's boy. Did Targ know that because the chairman of the philosophy department was leaving to be president of a medium-sized, semidenominational college, another department had fallen into their hands? They would fuse philosophy and classics (fuse? lose the classics department, Targ thought) into the stages section, for wasn't classics a stage on the critical path too? Targ should be its head; he was that distinguished; he was that well known. Or did it mean he had not joined the wrong clique, nor had he contended futilely, but was pleasing to all? What could it mean, more: that he angered the wrong people, published in the right journals three times a year, was invited to the right conferences all over the world, was a good infighter, a consultant, and had written one brilliant and one mediocre book, and performed his extracurricular duties with a kind of expedient verve? He had played his hand brilliantly in the days of the dissolution, maintaining a revolutionary, modernist, relevantist stance while preserving what had to be preserved: that wouldn't be forgotten. With a full managership, of course, *and* the raise in salary, to be sure. *And* a better house,

Colonial, without a doubt. Step up toward the key position in the New University, sitting astride a large chunk of the communications and simulations network.

Targ sat there. Ages went by as though they were but a second to him who had the sense of the Grand Sweep on the Grand Stage of History. Targ tried to say "No," but the chancellor went on to tell him what the duties would be, what new reprogrammings were to be set up, and how this was, for Targ, he felt, the grand opportunity to more than progress: to triumph.

And at that salary . . . Targ thought, and trembled.

But no, Targ thought, no, and no, not at all. The chancellor's vague smile showed that he didn't seem to hear Targ and, indeed, Targ wondered if he had even said anything. The chancellor only nodded benevolently and continued to watch the unpeopled pageant of history through the lancet window with its proscenium of ritualistic ivy, while the smell of roses along the walls, the humid scent of rot and hot vegetation rusting, the rustle of perpetual and riotous rut all along that teeming brick and marble wall kept coming in strongly.

There seemed to be no question of not taking it. None at all. But to show the chancellor his independence, Targ farted. The chancellor fixed his eyes upon the Stage of History determinedly and refused to look away, his dim eyes more suited to Grand Movements, Cycles, Scope, accretions of statistics; he chose to interpret the stage business, that fat, derisive flutter of the pants, as the creaking of a chair: such obscenities not being accounted for in his history. The chancellor took Targ's silence for assent and together they contemplated the precious moment. Then Targ got up to leave. The stench was strong—the food in the faculty cafeteria was faulty—and he reinforced it two or three times. The chancellor put it down to the incontinence of passion. He, the chancellor, who had seen the whole of mankind pass before his entertainment-mad eyes, who had contemplated all those billions of dying generations and smelled the collective stench of such moments, chose not to hear, or smell, him.

"I think I need vacation," said Targ.

"Well, if you must."

"I must."

"Rest and rehabilitation? Well, it has been a hard campaign, but we've stood off the assaults of the laity . . . in fact, won when we seemed to be losing. Up to the magic mountain and then back down to the plains to fight again?"

"Something like that."

"Well, everything's under control now. Why not?"

"I need it."

"I won't forget your part in all this, Targ."

"It wasn't much."

"It was. Targ, we needed new blood. None of us could have seen it that way in sixty-seven. None of us would have dared to say it even if we saw it. You had a different vision, or at least spoke it right out. You know, I once wondered what it was that old Biddle saw in people like . . . well, you. I'll admit it. I wondered why he brought you up—"

"Like a venerable Beatrice."

"So to speak . . . But that night I *knew*. You were almost one of us."

Almost? Not yet? On the other hand, the chancellor had not had his usual tongue slip and called him "Trag."

"Listen. Take a vacation in the Cradle of Civilization. Do the perimeter of the Mediterranean. Browse among the roots. Touch sacred ground, all the bases. Get revivified. You know, as a matter of fact, a new island has risen in that First Sea . . . or rather it is an ancient island rerisen. Terminus. You might look at it. Has some fascinating antiquities, I'm told. The natives are a little squeamish about digging and, I think, the French hold it. Old man Malraux and his penchant for hoarding. A complicated situation. It could definitively restore the Mediterranean again as the place where it all began. It might amuse you."

The chancellor's voice had the slight ring of command in it. Was this another test? I won't, he thought.

The voiding of poisonous gases had made Targ hungry, panicky, and trembly. He went home.

"You didn't do that, that farting, Targ, you didn't," Helen said.

If I didn't, then what are you doing here? he thought one last time before he gave in. "I did."

"But he didn't change his mind?" she asked.

"What difference?" Targ asked. "He had me a long time ago." And you had me too, he thought. But I accepted—I accept—forever.

"Don't talk nonsense, Targ. You're not feeling well."

"Don't worry about it, my love. You've brought me through. You're to bring me all the way."

"Can you hold on till the end of the semester?" she asked.

"I'll try," Targ said.

"I have an idea. Targ, we'll go abroad."

She too? "Indeed we will."

"We'll go to . . . Greece. You'll see. You'll feel better."

"A cruise cures, of course, all curses," Targ told her and tried to hold on to what he had almost forgotten.

2

Sunlight, a drink, a four-thousand-mile flight finally ended his fear. The dark edges were dispelled. At last he was a man merely sitting with his wife. His argument had the dimensions of a simple family quarrel, fiercely whispered so that all the other fiercely whispering tourist couples would not hear. It was now a quarrel that had no more stature than "Where shall we go, what shall we see next, what shall we photograph?" Pictures for the autumn shows of antiquities to the other teachers, who would, in turn, show them their slides. "And here is the sea of Marmara, gleaming like a jewel, surrounded by its green setting. And Byzantium." (They never called it Istanbul or Constantinople.) Family. Friends. Interesting travelers. Boat. Click. Temple. Whir. Water. Peasant. Click. Land. Whir. Gull. Click. Whir. Blackness. Click.

"I'm not reasonable," Targ told Helen.

"I know you're having a hard time, Targ." Her hand, essence of bronze, wide-palmed and long-fingered, of the Western blond-haired quite competent goddess variety, rested on the small tin table. An umbrella-topped pole popped right through the green center. The bay appeared to lie just below, lapping the edge of the terrace. But really the water was a few hundred feet down and a half mile out. Birds . . . gulls . . . unbirdlike gulls floated as if *on* it; wide-winged, hanging immured in the sky, which was, because of the Mediterranean light, so bright, shading off to cobalt. Her finger was sected with a gold band. It twitched with eagerness to make the leap of faith across the tin disk and touch his own, but didn't dare. I've done that to her, Targ thought, robbed her of their all-conquering sureness. He clinked the ice to answer her. Her burnished hair (Must he always use such words? he thought, exasperated: burnished was for leaf-cutting swords of the Greeks against the Trojans—or was it piercing swords against the leaf-shaped cutting swords; superior, to be sure; the wrath of Achilles, more meaningful and more overpowering because the iron age had entered his soul—against the gentle bronzite Priam and his loin fruit) . . . "Stop," Targ said.

"I'm sorry," she said. Her burnished face, fine-boned in the Anglo-Saxon way, was clear of the golden hair. Could Targ want for more? Gray-eyed like Athena, clear of troubles too. His dream-girl type when he first went to school. His first wife had been short, dark, tough, and couldn't get the ghetto out of her speech. Couldn't? Wouldn't. She would intercept his sly glances and monitor his secret life.

And he was annoyed at her because she didn't understand that he didn't mean her. Two tourists, wearing awning stripes, leaned, farther on, over the rococo balustrade and snapped pictures of the bay. Targ calmed himself by looking at the bay photographed, the sky photographed, the gulls photographed; at the green metal disk with a prickled Crete-shaped rough spot beneath the green enamel slick (perhaps a burn) over which the umbrella made a cone of shadow that did not include the strong hand he used to like to have touch him. He once found comfort in these things; he once found warmth in them. A race of conquerors served the conquered through her.

The day's newspaper was folded open on his lap, but there was no point to looking at it. French doom, Israeli doom, Arab doom, American doom, Greek doom, Bulgarian doom (or, from another point of view, Thracian doom); Babylonian and Berlin communiqués announced (brick leaves, cuneiform doom notes, too heavy to read in comfort) that the end of the world might come soon. Mass starvation. Total war. He slid the bottom of his glass across the tabletop. It rasped a little on the grained paint, making a rough sound, grinding glass and paint prickles down through the green, spreading out (as promising, nonobjective forms) a slick of water around. A tourist took color shots of his wife's white skin, limning freckles in turn framed by red hair against the sea; heavy jaws, eyes squinting, vertical wedge marks stamped on his low brow by the sun's intensity. Then the wife photoed his florid face and bright Italian shirt against the sky. Six Germans, militant in shorts, marched by, doggedly seeing the sights, firing salvos of camera clicks as they went.

He saw her glance. The old man passed during their third drink. Helen was impatient to go but, ministering love to the sick husband, sat stiffly posed in the position of relaxation, one bag-strapped, sun-browned shoulder against and over the back of the chair. Targ could see the muscles in her arm, her tennis arm. Mediterranean women were not like that at all. Given time, progress, the amusement industry, universal food packaging, Mediterranean women would become like Helen; selective adaptation. Her look was almost a nod. The old man duck-footed, waltz-walked across the terra-cotta *terrazzo*. Targ said, "Why, there's Professor Biddle!"

"I thought we'd escaped them all," Helen said, then asked, "Who's he?"

"We can never escape our fate," Targ said petulantly. "You, of all people, know that. Why do you ask such things or, for that matter, expect them?"

She nodded; her lips set a little; she bore with it; she salvaged, with love and eternal patience, their compact. She prepared her bright smile of welcome, as any faculty wife should, showing fascination for whatever calculus of specialization the mysterious and not yet known Professor Biddle might have. Who knew what that man might be able to do for Targ someday? Targ thought: I trained her that way. I am always destroying what I love. Guilt made him forget that perhaps she had trained him.

"Professor Biddle," Targ called. He told her—but not in words because there was too much to tell, and to talk about anything was too much trouble—Biddle had started him on the Path. Was it twenty years ago? He had said to Targ, a come-from-the-war sophomore, ". . . the cradle of civilization," negating for him all great holocausts with those grand words. Grand words delivered in the grand style, with a dignity that was of another age, an age Targ had since learned to identify as Victorian and treat (since he identified it) with scorn. But Professor Biddle had said, "Why are you here?" (And all these years, disturbed and restless hours and fears and not-feeling hadn't really expunged the reflex magic those beginning words evoked, only given them a somewhat sardonic tinge.) "Not the mere being in this classroom, but something greater and beyond, all of it, of this hour, of this now . . . When you were admitted into this university (and the getting in was not easy), when you stepped into this classroom (though many were called, few were chosen), you were committed to save Western civilization without even knowing what it was you were saving, not even knowing you wanted to save what you did not know; for, being *of* it, *in* it, *born* of it, you could not perceive it. From here we will escape it, go outside it, evert it, turn center into periphery, survey it from afar, as from a mountain"—later he would use the word "satellite"—"and begin to understand it." Then Professor Biddle had pointed out the window to the Corinthian-corniced chemistry building, the Medusa-topped pediments of a far-off factory, the superclassic lines of the Second Bank of the United States. "You are here because of *them; these* are there because of *them.*" The grand and arrogant dignity of it was beyond damage of time or foolishness, or so Professor Biddle thought. So Targ became a teacher of history; antiquities; Sumeric to Hellenic; Hellenic washing off the shit of Anatolian Cybelic rites.

"Who's he?" she asked in a quick little politician's whisper, already smiling that well-trained and lovely smile that was, Targ knew, half the reason to advancement to full professorship, chairmanship at so early a time in life. I'm not being fair, Targ thought. But then, even though they had met in college, and he had left his wife for what she represented, he had never really told her about old Biddle. A curious reticence. Old Biddle's boys talked about the Master to disciples only. They kept old Biddle a kind of secret. Most women were out; especially wives. Perhaps it was because of the sense that old Biddle imparted: they were a secret elect in a secret war, busily defending and extending their sector. "Professor Biddle the magician. He infers worlds from a horse's nail; and from the radioactive deposits on the insides of terra-cotta chamber pots, the contribution of the little man in heat to the imperial rut."

"Don't they all?" Helen asked.

Targ waved again and called to the arrested, bewildered figure standing helpless in the harsh sunlight. Biddle peered. Targ hadn't seen him for more than ten years. Biddle had aged and couldn't remember who Targ was. Or perhaps he had failed old Biddle in some way . . . some subtle test he had failed. What voice called from the solid umbra beneath the striped umbrella?

Professor Biddle advanced and stood there in the light, peering. His long body cringed as in a needle shower of heat. His shadow was quite small underneath his feet, as if he stood on his shadow's shoulders. He leaned on a thick-shanked cane that tapered to a solid point, ferrule-bound; his hands, old man's hands, trembling (he had been old even then, Targ remembered; he was beyond time now, retired, noodling around old antiquities before he died and became interred as a framed divinity—minor, very minor, of course—with professorial robes and the abstracted look of a sightless agonist), were closed one on top of the other on top of the carved cane knob.

"I beg your pardon," the man said. Targ saw that it was not Professor Biddle at all: how could it be? Professor Biddle should have been dead many years. Reason demanded it.

Targ started to turn away. Helen kicked him under the table. Targ rose. Helen leaned forward to show the old man her wonderful face, her fine smile. Targ made apologies; remarked that the resemblance between Professor Biddle and . . . ?

"My name is Kairos."

The resemblance was uncanny, and they must, laughing at the mistake, invite the man to sit with them. The old man swept off his hat and bowed. The sun poured on the almost bald head with its one thick, lush forelock, looking quite out of place on that old head, so shiny you wanted to grab it. Mr. Kairos sat, half in shadow and half in light, on one of the wire-and-rattan chairs. They creaked to comfort again, resuming positions: Helen's hand on the green tabletop, Targ's hand sliding the glass. Mr. Kairos, his hands folded on the gargoyle cane knob, teetered back and forth, bones, rattan, and wire creaking rhythmically as he talked.

Urbanely he offered Helen a cigarette. "Argive Helen?" he asked, and laughed. His voice crackled at the academic joke, long made, perfunctorily delivered, like crumpling paper. "I'm a businessman," he said. "Retired. Actually history has always been my real love. Argive Helen?" he asked again. Massachusetts Bay Helen, Targ thought. She laughed easily, wonderfully, as if hearing this *mot* for the first time, gentle and interested in this relic's wit.

Boston Helen, Leda's daughter, rape-engendered by swan-beaked papa the banker in a shower of gold. Only in this version Helen abducts Paris, he thought.

"No, thank you," she said, refusing the offer of the cigarette. "I prefer one of those tough little Greek ones." What did that mean?

Targ wondered. And if she cut at him, or if Targ's feelings found in her innocent remarks, such as they were, some hurtful meaning, he had it coming. Targ remembered for a second, and shuddered; but he was really all right now and they were having a fourth drink—Mr. Kairos's first—and it was all right, definitely all right.

"I am not one for many things American anymore," Mr. Kairos told Helen. "I have been abroad now for a long time. But as for cigarettes, that is one of the great cultural achievements the Americans have made." He laughed; the pied backs of his hands jiggled on the cane's knob.

"And the other is toilets, of course?" Targ said. Helen looked at Targ. She was right. Why take it out on this wreck? But Mr. Kairos laughed and said it was all right.

". . . once worked for the Old firm of Zaharoff and Gulbenkian, then I became a Merchant of Light"—he giggled—"for General Electric . . . and so I decided that as soon as I could I would leave business and go all over the world and see all the wonderful things: cathedrals, relics. . . . I was here in this city once, in 1939, but then the war . . . Zaharoff and Gulbenkian . . . I've read a lot in my time: biographies, histories, books on archaeology. I like to read historical novels; feel those people . . . have imaginary conversations with them," Mr. Kairos said. He had a curious way of talking, stopping as if waiting for some response beyond casual yeses, noes, nods, and not getting it. Helen was bored; the fixedness of her smile showed Targ that. Mr. Kairos dropped facts like a bright boy impressing his elders and Targ listened, nodded respectfully, acting as though enthralled, and knew how much each eager "Really, sir?" cost Helen in energy. "He knows quite a lot," Targ said to Helen.

"I wouldn't say that," Mr. Kairos said.

"Oh, much more than I," Targ said. "And I teach it."

Helen looked at Targ and said, "Oh, Targ," sadly.

They sat there for a while. Tourists passed. Mr. Kairos fiddled with matches, his cane top, and asked how long they had been there. Almost cross-eyed, bland, innocent; the manner of command had been worked into his common addresses, but was so useless, so foolish in this casual age. Targ remembered Professor Biddle, the academic jokes, the laughter, the long rolling periods reinforced by the momentum of all the years of teaching; a manner which indicated that he was ancient and wiser than anyone else, and certainly entitled to use the grand style. And after all, hadn't he also been an adviser to statesmen?

Targ said that they had just come that day.

From where?

From nowhere in particular.

Mr. Kairos wore a suit of some kind of clownish summer polyesters, as if that garishness, like an incognito, represented the wild inner man that had been forced to behave as routinely as postures painted on a vase.

Professor Biddle had once had an older sister, unmarried, but with a tongue as sharp as Xanthippe's; and even though they all loved old Biddle, they used to say he Orested'ed her Electra and that anyway the incest was practically classic. But she had died and released him from his posture.

Perhaps that was the reason for the wild polyesters. Release. The light fell in patches on Mr. Kairos's suit, the mottled green and yellow was not so much soiled or crumpled, but its material played tricks with light. Its garishness and the wide red paisley tie showed he had shucked off *his* Electra after all. He wore a drooping Schweitzer mustache which, gray and ragged, faded into his pouchy cheeks, falling over his mouth so that nothing of his lips showed but the center of the full, moist lower lip, trembling and shining and almost purple in the light. Now and then the click and clack of false teeth was manifest. "Of course, there is nothing to see in this city anymore. It is all becoming very concrete and steel; to be sure, very modern, very beautiful, very American, progressive, but very effectively buries the past, sir, don't you think, madam?"

Though Professor Biddle might have said the very same thing, Mr. Kairos, atoning for his commercial past, overworked his rejection of the businessy present. But after all, Greeks, Phoenicians, Hebrews had been traders, misers, and sneaky politicians too; builders of temple banks, Targ thought.

"Our heritage, our gift, our beginnings," Targ said. Helen agreed with Mr. Kairos and deplored the antiseptic lines and the light-swallowing dark metal skins. They had been all over the city trying to see something interesting that morning, but there was nothing left. Even their world-famous slum—a ghostlike concretization of all slums, back to the earliest of times—had been destroyed a long time ago. Whatever else looked interesting was interred in the museums. Le Corbusier, Nervi, variants of that cold kind of thing were being put up all over. Steel and glass; clean lines; white painted concrete: another classic city—already as dead as any of them—rose beside the blue, shining sea. Targ must have shuddered because Mr. Kairos asked, "Are you cold?"

Heat-absorbing buildings leave chills, Targ thought. The icy and nacreous light that illuminated and neutralized the incandescent shards in clean lined cases in the classics department iced Targ. Targ shook his head. "They are leveling the past, wiping out the scene of the great crimes, hiding behind neutral and abstract façades," Targ said. Helen looked at Targ as though he had intended to insult her: her past: of them born. But, not sure, she decided to bear it.

"And *there* is something that will level the past too," the old man said indignantly, pointing at Targ's newspaper. New nations had started bomb testing again. Pollution was eroding the most sacred relics. The price of preservation was being undercut by energy prices. Framing a tiny picture of a white and cottony puff (as stylized as a papyrus column, repeated till it was now almost a cliché, but still deadly enough) was a larger picture of the raging, indignant face of that newest mad modernized gnome, a modern Alberich, who faced another picture, of an American athletic leader who, with jaw outthrust and with his clean-cut aggressive innocence mask, seemed to wear his own little puff burst, in an inset, like a white boutonniere on his lapel. And below that a small gallery of those leaders who belonged to what they called the nuclear club, and the oil-producing club, and the energy-consuming club, and the food-producing club. "It pounds and it pulverizes and renders all to glowing dust," Mr. Kairos said. It was said as Professor Biddle might have said it. And once those words, said that way, would have been equal to about any one fact, but not to that truth in the paper. In the newspaper it added up to hopelessness; in Mr. Kairos's mouth the words were rodomontade, an old fool's bombast. What he didn't understand was the fact that the war had gone on for forty years and was almost over. Nothing was left.

Now Helen looked chilled. She dreamed about it. If they had children . . . if . . .

"We don't," Targ always told her. "And we did anyway," meaning their students. "We won't. Biology is no longer important; you know that. Extrauterine with monitored, selected genes; removing a bit of the mother sea into sterile caldrons," he had said. "The best of all possible combinations." She herself was a combination, a composite, a post-Byzantine mosaic, an assemblage of programs, urges, treasures; a lovely anthology.

"So what?" Targ asked and looked at Helen. She looked away, trying to keep up the fiction of love, politeness, and forgiveness for Targ's terrible moments of aberration. He had learned his consolatory lessons well. Man is destructive naturally. Empires rise and fall. These things have always been. History progresses by its bad side. Progress is inevitable anyway . . . at some costs. What was required was that history be made cost effective. Everything will come out all right. The fine disregard on God's part is for men, not the race. Why worry: in the midst of such splendor, while acting like happy and oblivious tourists taking trips on installment plans, why worry? The ice of his drink clinked against the bite of his teeth.

But Mr. Kairos chose not to hear Targ. Like Professor Biddle on the rostra of a thousand classrooms (or a thousand organization meetings), he orated and ended periods glowingly. ". . . and we can go nowhere without having that thing alongside, do nothing without the memory of it, and yet we must go on. What did you say?"

"Yes. It's a threat to national monuments . . ."

"I don't think that's funny, sir," Mr. Kairos said.

". . . and renders all the present, and this present past, a more ancient and pluterperfect past than the Valley of the Kings, sir." Targ saw that it bothered Helen and continued to mock.

"People . . ."

". . . don't care or think about it," Targ said. "It will happen." Targ saw the corners of those gray eyes of hers crumple just a little, as though she had been pinched. "Perpetual peace is a dream, and not even a beautiful dream," Targ said to annoy them.

". . . are suffering," Mr. Kairos finished.

"The world is a great tomb," Targ said. She smiled, but she was hurt. He could feel the anxiety beginning to return. Her eyes looked at Kairos as if to apologize. Volumes passed between them. Kairos nodded and shrugged.

Mr. Kairos stopped. He thought. He nodded to himself, to Helen, as if making up his mind. Yes. He produced a little brochure. It was shiny, sleazy, a little greasy to the touch, like the rotogravure sections of Sunday papers. "There," Mr. Kairos said, pointing to the centerfold. "Now *that* is something." Targ picked it up and looked at the picture. The anxiety was definitely returning; he thought it was ridiculous because it was, after all, daylight. And yet he couldn't help feeling excited by the picture. One side had printing in three languages—Russian, English, and Indo-European—in a narrow column. The teeth of the type seemed not to have gripped the slick paper; hesitated and bit again so each letter was duplicated, not so much side by side but as an imperfect superimposition that almost obscured what was said. Reading it made the eyes ache. Helen leaned closer over the table, on Targ's side, trying to read what it said. Targ smelled her. American soap and cleanliness in spite of Europe. Saw a flash of hair wave and the pothook curve of her ear. Brown skin and neck muscle to be bitten . . . But he leaned away. On two-thirds of one side and sweeping through the center staples and all over the other side was one picture. It showed a perfect little Greek temple, perfect as much as if it were an architectural illustration, drawn rather than photographed. "Visit Terminus," the brochure said trilingually. Targ sweated even though he sat in the cone of shadow. He remembered the chancellor's advice. "I've had enough of the classic past, thank you," he told Mr. Kairos. Targ could see Helen's warning look. Advice, request, or order? He turned away and stared out over the sheet of bay.

"But who can have enough?" Mr. Kairos asked.

"I can."

"Then you've seen *everything?"* and he cackled. Helen laughed with him so he wouldn't sound foolish.

"Enough samplings to represent everything."

"But such beauty . . ."

"Sticks up from the burial ground."

"The classic past"—he made the words ring—"implies, to be sure . . ."

Targ decided to be immune to this old fool. "Just a few more spadefuls." Or was it spadesful? Targ wondered.

". . . perfection forever wherever one goes, but this is *so* beautiful that . . ." and he laughed. Targ heard the sound of a pillar tearing loose and falling; the incredible sound of phlegm tearing and rattling in Mr. Kairos's throat while his eyes remained so anxious to persuade him.

"It's really one of the most wonderful things I have ever seen," Helen said. She would keep Mr. Kairos from knowing as long as possible. She was good that way. Targ would have him know as soon as possible, without telling him directly. He had had it with the past. Then it became a silent game between the two of them, Targ and Helen, and the closer Targ came to telling Mr. Kairos what was wrong, the more he hurt Helen and the more she resisted his telling. How much could she take? Leave me, he thought. Her eyes remained calm, gray, but that long-preserved youth, that beauty of hers, had been decaying slowly through the months: crinkles at the sides of the eyes appeared; set-mouth wrinkles in the cheeks, a realism not practiced by the Greeks or the Egyptians. Did hidden spots beneath the blond-brown of her hair metamorphose into gray? Targ wondered.

"Spadesful," Targ said, making up his mind. But, he thought, what she said *was* true. Being a color print and so having the imperfections, or rather the overperfections, color prints had, it was nevertheless wonderful. The sky was pure blue, although there was something burned-looking about it. The temple was regular, perfect in its way, small. It was on a hill that was too green; Astroturf. But that was the fault of the panchromatic coloring too.

"And if you look hard, you can just see the island. Do you have good eyes?" Mr. Kairos asked. "The weather's perfect." His eyes were an old man's eyes: gray, watering just a little, with red veins on buff-colored eyeballs. Thick pouches surrounded the squint whose rays dented the finer wrinkled skin of the eyelids, tightly drawn beneath the raised, high-arched brows, so bushy and white. In Professor Biddle that would have been a noble look, Targ thought. In Mr. Kairos it was almost sly, comic, conspiratorial. Mr. Kairos pointed out toward the bay and beyond, where the sea seemed to thicken a little in one spot.

"I see it. It's beautiful," Helen said.

"I'm just a brown-eyed boy among the gray-eyed wise. Different gene pools. Training conquers optics," Targ said. She looked at him and seemed to see into him. She showed him that what she saw didn't revolt her. "I see a smudge," Targ had to say to admit to her she had won a bargaining point. He was honorable and negotiated in good faith. "A wrinkle . . . a pucker."

"It is there," Mr. Kairos said.

What was smoke and air out there, Targ thought (was he drunk so early in the day), had been transferred and condensed to reality in the form of the print underneath the tapping of Mr. Kairos's finger on the paper or, as now, was deceptively immutable on the glossy blue sky beneath the tapping of their eyes. Targ could, accepting what they saw, imagine a gull sweeping slowly across the sky, going in and out behind the temple pillars; he could just smell the nitrate freshness of the too green grass, see the ocean beyond; almost feel the warm sun on the marble which looked, in the unfortunately superperfect photo, a little too warm, somehow plastic.

"I was there once before the First World War and again in August of 1939. I was working for Zaharoff and Gulbenkian then; grand old firm. I came on a business mission and stayed to love the place. I'm afraid I sold nothing."

"I thought this island has just risen from the sea."

"Where did you hear that?"

His heart began to pound faster. Why?

"I have been touring the Continent and Africa and Asia for years; and the years have taken me eastward. And all this time I have been wanting to get back to the island again. I keep forgetting particulars —senility, you know, Mr. Targ: the price of getting old—everything but the feeling I had for the place. And how do you describe a feeling?" And Mr. Kairos laughed, making Targ laugh too. Helen didn't laugh but watched them both carefully. "But it is the last thing I want to see before I go back to America to die: I must die in America. A ferry goes there every other day."

"All right." Targ sighed. "It *is* something. But the picture is probably better than the reality."

"No. No. I remember . . ."

"And memory is better than the picture," Targ told him. He felt again a touch of something chill, something producing a cold sweat (or was it merely the hard shadow of the umbrella?). And he could feel Helen being concerned. She missed nothing. No, her love made her miss nothing. What did she love? Targ wondered. (He knew.) Don't love, he thought at her. "Like the Parthenon is supposed to be." Or was he chilled because a little sea wind's sweep up the hill was iced in passage by the white houses and the chill blue sky?

"Ahhhhh . . . the Parthenon." And every word was underlined by the raising of that old voice into a senile coo. They always went

into raptures about the Parthenon . . . that or something they discovered that no one else knew about, which was better than—but always in relation to—the Parthenon. "But surely, don't you care for the Parthenon?" Mr. Kairos was hurt.

"The trouble is that the mind's eye, already educated, trained, long expectant, is full of worship and overcompensation . . . or fills in what is not there and probably never was there. I first saw it when I was in college. The Periclean Greeks would have laughed themselves silly at what *I* saw," Targ told him. Targ saw it for what it was now, no longer with the eyes of tradition, freed from Byron's, Goethe's, and old Biddle's romantic enthusiasms, not with the wishful eye that canceled out reality, delivered from the tyranny of Greek revivalists. This trip, hard sunlight had rendered it flat, dusty, jumbled, inconsequential. This time there was the junta . . . but then he realized that other individuals—another junta—had been there when they had built it. And that sky—usually too blue, too hard—was white and out of it poured intolerable light. Targ wondered if they had come at the wrong time of the year. He tried to recapture the sense of it, the sense he had on other trips. He was tempted to feel it through Helen. But he was on guard. She felt what she was supposed to feel. Her very name was against her. She had grown up, the whole sense of her senses assembled of these (and other) traditions. She was their eyes and their emissary, perceiving only visions her equipment could perceive, altering reality with the passage of the seeing through her: she was a semiconductor. Give in to her vision and he was lost, for she was not yet totally his wife. So all he could see was the crumbled masonry, the eaten-away pillars, the shattered shafts and entablatures. Targ tried harder. The sweat poured out of him. He only remembered words: "The cultural achievements of the Greeks"; a name or two, and those most banal, common at that. Aristotle, another silly fag, Plato, Alcibiades; a god or hero or two: Dionysus, Apollo, Hermes the great spy, Zeus; marble horse-crest helmets, throwing spears, blind blank eyes, and broad brows. . . . The furious and petulant political quarrels of playwrights and philosophers struggling for the dominance of their ideas, sucking up to the powerful, willing, all, to alter their theories for a few drachmae, throwing out lofty ideas while pinching the arses of young boys, pumping their pricks like handles on old computers while out came memories of Leibniz's calculus.

Dust and bird shit lay over all. Below the Acropolis there was a jumble of terrifying slums. Stupid, brutal country boys in uniform were everywhere, watchful now of the too verbal, the too effete. Spies were everywhere, preserving that republic. Television aerials and cook smoke curling upward.

"But did you see it by moonlight?" Victorian old Biddle-Kairos asked. "Sometimes the jaded vision can be cured by seeing it in the moonlight." And Mr. Kairos's voice went up the register again, rhapsodizing. ". . . looked at it many times . . . and sat under the pillars . . . yielded to the spell and felt the stream of history flowing and entering me and somehow curing me of depressions and glooms."

Targ almost asked, "Do you really believe that shit?" but he would have lost the game. Mr. Kairos's eyebrows went higher, to express rapture, Targ supposed . . . that or, because his face was in the cone of shadow thrown by the umbrella, Kairos was trying to see Targ more clearly. Mr. Kairos kept talking about the thrill he had had . . . how many times had it been? Did it ever stop!? How many times more? Mr. Kairos had not much time and would really like to see it again, have that thrill of sitting by the Parthenon by moonlight, midnight to be exact. Of course, Targ thought, of course; it had to be midnight to get the full historical flavor of it. Pay the entrance fee for *Walpurgisnacht.*

But rather, Targ remembered unwillingly, it had been different for him. Targ had got out of bed. Helen didn't say anything even though she was awake at Targ's slightest move (she was a good and loving nurse). One great argument had fixed that; she left him alone because to love is to accept, no matter what wild aberration . . . Yes . . . he had turned her own weapons on her. Targ went to the Acropolis alone. The moon was shining. He stood there. He tried to feel what all the classical revivals had felt—Medieval, Renaissance, German, English, French, American—but it fell apart into planes, varying areas of black and bluish darkness, rectangles, triangles, long areas permeated by stone and mortar dust, contradicted by a little realistic night damp, possibly dew. Professor Mingus of the art department would just love this; he painted à la Mondrian. (The Museum of Modern Art had a Mingus; David Rockefeller had had him to tea.) Old Halliday, the socialist realist, the strike and poster painter who had been driven into abstract expressionism after the Second World War, would hate it. But Targ's heart began to pound a little harder and it was not a matter of confirming old academic arguments any longer—since the academy in that sense was dead—and there was no longer an art department; students lazily created with computerized laser holographs. . . .

He felt as though there was something he had forgotten. Perhaps an important appointment. Something he was supposed to do. But he had no appointment. He had nothing but time, endless time; at least until autumn, when the school semester began again. If he wanted to, Targ could have sat on some squat column chunk till morning came and reddened (he supposed, but he was no longer sure) everything, or leave right then. But anxiously, as if he had to pass some important examination, as if he had to place things, identify them, he tried to remember what he had forgotten . . . and that was the worst thing of all to do. He could only remember the feel of smooth paper, such as is found in textbooks (and those the most elementary texts of all), something saying: "The Greeks of the Periclean age constructed with curved lines so as to give the illusion of straightness," and while that statement refuted Mingus, and certainly Halliday, it made Targ more anxious. He was in a hurry and he didn't know why (old Kairos's ecstatic voice droned on; Helen's clear contralto, loving and reasonable, counterpointed Kairos: they merged into a conspiratorial and annoying hum), because it was a calm and moonlight air (and so he reached out to touch reality, the flat surface of the tabletop, to feel); he felt a texture of prickles and crumbled surface, a little like the imperfect atomic flitter beneath (the green enamel surface of the table; Kairos's voice kept extolling) those classic perfections. The blood pounded in his ears and he thought: One, if Halliday and Mingus were wrong, Kolbasy, the action painter, was right, and, two, he had to run away from all this. Don't run, Targ told himself, because he would break his neck on all this massive inconsequence. The pounding concentrated in his heart and from there, radiated outward, shook his whole body and Targ thought it was happening again. The areas dissolved further to black and white, smudges, less meaningful, and then the pulse in his head throbbed into headache and the great, flaring moon smudges dissolved all to gray, universal gray. He held it back for a second by chanting catch phrases. . . . No, it was happening because of the Turks; the Turks did it. They shot up the Acropolis because it was used for a munitions dump . . . then it was really the fault of the Greeks for provoking the Persians, but now, for the time being, they were being protected by the Americans. ("I saw it," Targ told Mr. Kairos. "I saw it by moonlight.") And then he had to run and finally, banal phrases dripping from him like a litany of prayer, held everything together till he could get away from there. He said, ". . . and the Parthenon is the apotheosis of that Greek culture which has given rise to our democratic heritage."

"Yes," Mr. Kairos said.

He had run through the grayness till the ache in his heart and the pain in his lung became physical enough to substitute for the mental, restoring him to the feel of his feet on the road as he ran on and on. And when he came down to the twentieth century, he had to get himself drunk, get himself a whore, as garish as possible, whose accomplished artistry and sweaty acrobatics removed him from his fear finally.

When Targ came back to Helen it was morning. Keep loving me now, he thought-challenged, and hated her for being needed. Helen did; she kept on loving Targ. He could have wept, but instead he made caustic remarks to her. She was silent. She sat there and wore a white slip. Her long and slightly muscular arms were folded under her breasts, her long legs crossed at the ankles. She leaned forward while she watched him and loved him. All right, Targ thought, bear this, and entered her. And she bore him and loved him and, in spite of it all, he felt as though what they did was done not only through clothes, but through the skins the Acropolis dust and the whore's sweat had given him; he could have despaired that he felt nothing other than anxiety and anger, but fell asleep instead.

So much, he thought, for the Parthenon (and ordered a fifth drink).

He had to get out of Athens that day because wherever he turned he could see that horrifying unreality perched on that cliff. She said, "If you're in such a hurry, why don't we fly?"

"To fly would get us where we might be going too fast. Thus there is no sense of distance between here and there. Can you understand that?"

"That's not so hard to understand, Targ." Was there some harsh note in her voice? Had he won so easily? They left that afternoon.

They took a little coasting freighter. They went around the Peloponnesus, up the Adriatic to Trieste, to Venice, down the Adriatic to Brindisi, through the Strait of Messina, up the west coast of Italy, and from Genoa west. It took two weeks. But the sunlight had ended the fear and now, again, he felt nothing more than a little soothing anger.

"Then you know what I mean," Mr. Kairos said, and smiled through the fringes of his mustache. "Will you come with me?"

Helen's wisdom, compassionate, love-filled, obdurate, made her utilize a strategy of permissiveness. "Would you believe it, Mr. Kairos; we have been dragging around this continent from dig to dig, from national monument to national monument, and not once have I been to Paris." She laughed what she called her "foolish woman" laugh. Targ thought: Am I to be let loose at last? She said, "Now, why don't you two just go and look at this island together?" The foolish old Mr. Kairos, with old-world courtesy, insisted that she must come along. Laughing her simpering laugh, she told him Paris held monuments of a different nature. She would fly up, buy riotously, and fly back in time to meet them returning from the island. That meant she was sure of him now. The crisis was over.

Well, thought Targ, where could he run?

"I'm leaving him in your competent hands," Helen said. Those competent hands trembled a little. Delight or palsy? Targ wasn't sure which. Was Mr. Kairos seventy or eighty? He was as timeless as an ancient memory. Well, Targ thought, he was not fooled by the release act, and thought that right back at Helen. Her grip, though compassionate, though loving, was tough and held him at the end of its magnetic tether through space, through time. Helen's bright look pretended to innocence and fond adoration and Targ thought, almost weeping over that day's sixth drink: why didn't he treat her well; why didn't he love her?

That night she said, "Why do you torment that foolish old man?"

"He is old Biddle's ghost and doomed for a certain term—"

"I can't stand it."

Meaning it was all right if Targ tortured *her* but she buffered him from acting on the world. What mad god was Targ, to be stopped by her sad and loving domesticity from destroying it all? The woman's eternal brown and tennis-racket-gripping hand prevented, Targ thought.

"He knows more than I do now," Targ said.

"Oh, Targ," Helen said and cried a little and tried to hold him.

"But it is only temporary. The amateurs have it all now. I will remember, recapture it, and then let him watch out."

3

The ferry to the island was a converted fishing boat. Its auxiliary engine beat noisily from anapests to amphibrachs. There weren't ever many passengers who went to the island; the brochure after all attracted very few people. Targ and Mr. Kairos stood in the bow of the ship. It was a five-hour trip. Perhaps that was because it didn't go straight but made changes of course for no apparent purpose at all; as if trying to throw off a follower, which was ridiculous because the boat was too small and no one followed. Or perhaps it ran some complicated channel, although that too was silly since the boat had a very shallow draft. Targ watched, and could feel the prow lift itself high and throw itself down, splintering the smooth sea into waves whose revengeful and obdurate beat reciprocated against the wooden ship shell.

The sea was filled with white pleasure boats, multicolored yacht sails, the Russian Fleet and the American Sixth Fleet and a third major fleet—to say nothing of Italian, French, Turkish, Greek, Israeli gunboats. All beating aimlessly about. Some remained anchored to white sunbeams. Inevitable gulls accompanied, a little higher than the ferry's masthead; not so much flying as—still-winged, hanging—drawn through blue space by some invisible string tied from boat to bird. High above the gulls, contrails of warplanes sectored the skies into fantastic shapes. The farther from land they got, the heavier the air traffic. American planes played chicken of the sea with Russian warships, screaming down as close as they could, daring the Russians to shoot. The Russians held off firing, wondering if each shrieking dive-bomb run would be the real thing. Great Russian bombers, flying out of old Colchis across the Black Sea, would come in fast, as if to crash-land on American carriers, tracked by swiveling guns while on the vast decks men scrambled away from the almost sure crash; they would veer at the last moment and continue on toward Africa. The ferry passed a destroyer converted into a pleasure boat, on which there seemed to be a furious race of the naked going on all around the ship. It passed vast assemblages of landing boats, all filled with armed men, waiting in place, using only enough power to maintain their position. The sea and growing things had crusted and rusted their sides. How many years had they been there?

The island manufactured itself with each tack of the ship, overlay by overlay being lifted off, from smudge to shadow to solid, going from something distinct and dimly blue, but darker than the sea and sky, and darker still, into green punctuated by pink, white, gray squarish dabs: houses and roads. Behind them the mainland port fell away, its features negated one by one until it became all white, gleaming, attractive once more against the endless sweep of the land.

As they passed boats, sunburned people smiled hectically and waved. But Mr. Kairos kept peering at the island and saying, "Yes, yes, that's it, that's it."

Mr. Kairos stood beside Targ, telling him about the history of the island, relating it in great detail. The wind swept past them and picked at the loose white suit Mr. Kairos wore now, billowing the cloth like dirty sails, flinging the tie back like a paisley pennon. ". . . and of course they speak a Latinate tongue . . . somewhat like French; yes, that's it, mostly French, in honor of their most impressive conquerors. Charlemagne imposed one of his schools there. But then there are so many words that are pre-Latin, possibly Phoenician, possibly Basque, certainly quite ancient. Say a Latinate bêche-de-mer for the authorities, an officialese with the counterpoint of a guttural something which they talk among themselves . . . Do you think it could be Lithuanian?" Targ shrugged. Once he would have been excited; it no longer mattered. "Or Sanskrit. That would be exciting." Targ nodded yes. That would be exciting. "Or even Indo-European itself," and Mr. Kairos looked anxiously at Targ.

Targ squinted his eyes against the light as though debating it, as though having a moral conflict about it, and then nodded suddenly as if he had made up his mind. "Yes. Yes. That might be it," Mr. Kairos's voice mewled. "There is some debate about it. Their constructions are interesting too. They actually have, you know, more inflections than old Latin, Greek, or prehistoric Chinese. . . ." The gulls called to one another, three long shrieks conjugating down to a fourth sound, a squawk; one sat mockingly on the sea, a little to their side, just outside the rage of the waves the prow threw up. The engine beat clumsily, hammering out its monotonous rhythms.

Mr. Kairos kept extolling the island. Targ looked to the land, beginning to smell it out through the smell of sea, the fish smell that never washed off the ferry's railings, the smell of oil. The ship was entering the zone of reeks, donkey, goat, and man shit universally laid down to fertilize their soils. The island became greener; patches metamorphosed to visible buildings, mostly clumped at one end. Behind them, the port had diminished to a brilliant patch against the smoky mainland.

Mr. Kairos had begun to talk about his life. Targ turned for a second and saw Mr. Kairos's face at his shoulder. Mr. Kairos wasn't looking at the sea, the island, or the birds; he looked at Targ. The wind had cleared the moisture from his old eyes; they were now hard, gray, clear. Targ had trouble, for a second, looking at those eyes, but the soft pouches underneath made them look miserable, troubled, pleading. Mr. Kairos was saying something about wandering around the face of Europe, lonely, visiting sites where all the ancients had camped and where, now, the moderns were reopening all those ancient cesspools and shitpiles. Each discovery threw the history further and further back, shattering the sequence of progress and evolution. That bothered him. Cave paintings, as sophisticated as the European, had been found in Central Asia. Did that mean spontaneous creation, extensive world trade, or the collective unconscious? And what about evolution (they called it sequence and critical path operations these days)? The issue was in doubt. Some proposed Africa as the birthplace of man. Some Asia. That didn't matter so much. What mattered was *this* birthplace of civilization: that was at stake. And now they intruded the Celts: Stonehenge and Balbec older than Egypt? Ridiculous. Where would it stop? Three years Mr. Kairos had been wandering; Targ heard that. Mr. Kairos's face looked twisted and he opened his mouth wider and wider, trying to speak above the hiss of the water sliding past, the slap-boom of the water against the prow, the call of the gulls, the now steady and apparent beat of breaking waves against the shore, and the throb of the clumsy engine.

"So I thought it was a matter of having nothing to do that was getting me down. Well, sir, I said I would sit down and write a story of my life; a kind of cultural history of a businessman in love with the past . . . with art." And there was something longing in Mr. Kairos's eyes, something pained, anxious, something wanted from a stranger:

Targ. Targ didn't want to see it. He turned away a little, not enough to be impolite, kept nodding as though listening to Mr. Kairos, yet trying to see the scenery at the same time. . . . Who could blame him for that?

The island green looked lush. Fat bubbles floated by. The mast arced slowly to pitch and yaw above Targ's head. ". . . and I asked myself two things: how would this be different from any other biography . . . you know, 'Fifty Years, the Maxims of Success.' But for heaven's sake, I thought, although I have known literally thousands of people, where are the people in it, where are the people? I don't remember them at all. Brief business meetings, sometimes in the middle of the night; Venice, Genoa, Milan, Brussels, Damascus, London . . . and sometimes women . . . and moving on again. What have I done with my life? Have you ever wanted to write a book?"

Of course, Targ thought; but I'm writing it. And the sudden trickery of his sickness made truth flicker so that the rise and fall of civilizations, the grand sweep and the divine purpose across the stage of history meant nothing to Targ anymore. All dead. Stones. Fused glass. All coalesced in one flesh. Where were the people in it? Here was Kairos, one of the people, but . . .

Why is he telling me this? Targ wondered. What does he want? All he could seem to hear was the sound of Mr. Kairos's voice; all he could do was net the sense of it, sound and sense superimposed like unmatched printing. It ranged from nasal to moralistic to didactic to whining in its insistence. The face was screwed up with the pain of telling, as if he were about to cry. Old man, Targ thought, I have my own troubles . . . and as for people, what in the world are those? Esoteric boxes inside larger esoteric boxes. Targ looked at the island. It was nearer. Its pungency troubled his nose. The buildings were now gray, salt-stained. The once-seen-as-red roofs had faded into brown-pink. Behind the little village the island rose slowly to be gathered into a pale knot. That must be the temple, that perfect temple. Mr. Kairos kept telling Targ sad tales of his life, about his great love, the small but key moments in that life, opportunities not taken

—didn't it fit?—talking, putting out his hand, waving his cane, explaining himself, grimacing, which meant either a wry, ironic smile, or a look of ingratiation; Targ couldn't be sure which. Mr. Kairos was trapped, nevertheless, by the demands of forms of entertainment cultivated to catch the ears of the bored all over Europe: the way Professor Biddle wove, bound, knotted all those years of classes to the podia of classrooms, chained thousands with grand motions calculated to draw out the interests of students not interested. Now and then Professor Kairos turned as if making some aside to the sea (the way Mr. Biddle would make an aside to the boy always sleeping on the side of the room, or to some stupefied face staring out at a spring landscape, undaunted by chalk, wet slate smells, and history), the gulls, the engine, the dead-faced crew, the pleasure boats, the battle fleets, the scraps floating in the water. Targ saw that Mr. Kairos had old man's thick gray hairs growing from his ears and felt like laughing. Targ thought: You have been away from home a long time, for no American shrugs his shoulder that way, or puts his hands out in that gesture.

The ferry heeled broadside to the island. Its motor began to rev up to an unbearable pitch, shaking the boat, going faster and faster away from the town, but keeping an equal distance from the island, along some invisible circumference, then it seemed to turn, and yet not turn; a mass of spray higher than the masthead obscured everything, and the ship was headed in the opposite direction, as if the prow had flowed through the boat and out the stern, while the motor was suddenly silent. The boat turned toward the island and the motor resumed again. There were no ships here, as if they had passed around and through some invisible perimeter and entered a shipless zone.

Targ nodded sympathetically in time to the rhythms of Mr. Kairos's tone, but watched, rather, the blocks of white and gray, enjoying their sensual neutrality, watched the great green triangle the island made, the little tip of paleness at the top, and the slow and festive flight of little clouds overhead and the way high currents bowed the contrails into great circles. Mr. Kairos's history, a man come to his end, was finished, and so was the story of descent, or ascent, tragedy, whatever sad tale he had to tell. And that simply because those words no longer had any meaning. He waited for Targ to say something.

"Things like that happen all the time," Targ said. Mr. Kairos looked disturbed. "I mean it's life, Mr. Kairos. We're all in the same boat. Believe me." Mr. Kairos looked more disturbed and continued to talk.

The engine cut off suddenly. The ship was floating suspended over the shallow, transparent water, coming in, a momentum through air, to a long, half-crumbled wharf. Two or three of the natives were standing on the edge of things, waiting for them. Mr. Kairos's voice reemerged from the silence, pedantic, droning, but still with the same sense of weeping and anxiety in it, saying: ". . . and of course the island has been overrun time and again since the beginning of time. Indeed, no native has ever fought for the place. But always the conquerors have come in and, finding nothing of any worth, have stationed a corporal's guard here, who of course have nothing to guard except national pride. It cannot even serve as a good naval base. It has a poor harbor. Of natural resources it has none. Of food, home grown, there is merely enough, what with the fishing in the winter, of course, to feed the population; no more. When I was here first, the island was being held by the Church . . . uh . . . ah . . . I mean the League of Nations for the Spanish, the Italians, the Genoese, or the French, whoever it was decided exerted the strongest claim. There is no longer a League of Nations but a UN, and now it is the French, or is it the Spanish . . . ? Possibly. Well, at any rate, *they* hold the place."

The smell of droppings coming down from the land beyond the town was almost overpowering. On the other side of the wharf a long warehouse made of gray boards jutted out, set on pilings over the water. A few fishing boats were tied to the wharf. Farther up on the beach more fishing boats lay canted. The boats on the beaches peered up at the circling gulls and the web of contrails out of red eyes painted on their prows. As the ferry drew in, a wave slapped up between its side and a wharf piling, wetting Targ, forcing water into his nose. The water in spite of its transparency seemed dirty, somehow oily; Targ spluttered. Water burned Targ's eyes. Water wet Targ's hair. Water stuffed Targ's nose and ears. Mr. Kairos kept talking, lecturing about the island, and though it was no longer the story of his personal woe, he kept grimacing and appeared ready to weep. He would not notice Targ was wet. The boat had come to a stop about two feet from the wharf, suspended ten feet above sand, shells, a few starfish, and glittering debris. Ropes were thrown to the standers on the pier. Squat people, no taller than five feet four or five, but very broad, thick-boned, short-legged, long-torsoed, with, all of them, short, almost invisible necks and heavy sloping shoulders. The sun dried Targ quickly. They pulled the boat against the wharf till they had the side of it tightly warped against thick coils of half-frayed, half-rotted rope bumpers. Their faces had the kind of anonymity that men who work outdoors all their lives have: blank-looking in spite of the intense black eyes in the brown faces.

They got off the boat. The town was a small village of about fifty houses. There wasn't a hotel, but one house, a little larger than the rest, served as a kind of inn, or pension. They got two rooms on the top floor. Targ's room looked out over the sea, back toward the mainland. Targ could see a part of the island curving away and around to his left. The port lay straight ahead, beyond the belly of the land and over the flat sea. The sea was filled with boats of pleasure and battle. The beach was only a narrow strip, no wider than twenty feet, circling away, fading, the edges joining in the distance . . . a white and shining new-moon shape.

Only a wooden chest of drawers with ornately carved panels and a bed covered with a white sheet—no pillows—were in his room. There was a crudely baked and garishly colored earthenware pitcher and basin on the chest. Targ was restless. He couldn't stay long in his room. He put his suitcase down on the bed, opened it, and was going to change his clothes, but the clothes he was wearing had dried and it was too much trouble to undress and dress. It was getting late. The night was coming. The sun fused everything in a furious and garish red glare as it sank. Targ went downstairs without bothering to get Mr. Kairos, who he hoped was resting. Targ didn't want to listen anymore.

There was nothing to see in the town. The few houses, almost all alike; a rough, narrow road paved with stones set in the centuries-packed dirt; the one little café . . . Immediately outside the village the fields began. It was too simple and a little haphazard, the walls of the buildings not being lined up. The town's arrangement, if one could call it that, irritated him. Somehow it didn't fit. Fit what? Anthropologists' preconceptions? Circles arranged according to clans and moieties? Lévi-Strauss arrangements? And yet there was no sign as to why this street was where it was, other than that it was an extension of the wharf. But then why was the wharf there? Nothing natural had dictated this arrangement or, on the other hand, nothing unnatural.

Children, who all seemed to look alike, were playing obscure and ancient games in the short, one-house, one-block side streets. Women passing were mysterious in black, even though now, in all the villages around the Mediterranean, the poorest towns, cheap, gay, sacrilegious synthetic prints were winning out. The great two-thousand-year mourning was over. Mourning closed off all possibility. No sign of that here; not even an advertising poster. That the women still wore black showed how poor, or bound by custom, they were; their simplest acts were infected by thousands of years of repetition. Ritual was degenerated efficiency. All growing, gathering, carrying, eating, fucking, emptying, dying, burying, growing were imprinted by style and distorted.

They looked alike. An isolated and stagnant genetic pool, a kind of purity of type that how many centuries of isolation had developed, or failed to develop. Their very alikeness was exasperating: no admittance of any foreign sexuality (it excited him), indicating the miserly hoarding of energy in perfect circular flows.

Targ almost felt mean, excited now as he looked at these small, black-clad, dumpy but strong women. (His first wife would have turned out like this. He was sure of it. He consoled himself for his desertion of her by this sureness.) But was it all an illusion? Too much reading; associations of agriculture and agricultural rites; sex and obsessive behavior (and constant harvests) in daily life; closed, inviolate, and tabooed circles of people in events brought out . . . what? an irreverent tumescence in his groin and a tingling in his head. The mild excitement persisted in spite of his knowledge that he reacted to what they stood for, not what they were. But it was mild; he was losing his ability to get excited by the symbols for things, and as for the actuality the symbol pointed to, that had long gone, long gone. Too much belief, a trick of books and the conditioning through books and the learning to feel through books which refined and redefined the emotions . . . being possessed by the major and pervading accretions of classicists, ethnologists, anthropologists, and General Systems Evolutionists. He walked on, trying to believe he was still fascinated by acts and appearances long dead for him, as if he were decoding customs, finding still-living relics and natural rhythms compressed, treasured in a domestic or casual gesture (but knowing these to be the persistence of a now outmoded expediency), seeing statue poses in common pursuits, the sum of those poses another totality.

He remembered: a two-legged and four-armed two-headed being, all four hands dance-moving; each movement having its special arcane meaning; confronting and fusing with another two-legged . . . Targ and Trag, Helen and Trag's wife, and of these figures, Targ and Helen further linked, pulsating relay stations, fluid, bubbling into being and being reabsorbed . . . And then stopping because somewhere the integrative energy had been stopped. Where? Obdurate dumpy women in black, their very shortness/squatness a sign of their selfishness, self-containment, smugness, sufficiency . . . Hands dipping into a pâté dip, holding crusts of bread, dolloping the bread, passing to hand, anchovy curl, passing to hand, pimento centered, arcing to be placed on a large platter, and between movements interspersing caresses . . .

(Bas-relief on a statue of interlinked reliefs . . . Indian towers which seemed merely to be compendia of fuckings with their thousand positions of sex and love but represented the passage and exchange of energy, yes, sense the energy coming from the earth itself, flowing up to, gaining velocity, the tip —commandings of desire going from tip down to and into earth, flowing round and round in a winding spiral of stone, through the embracings of figures, its million components, positions, compilations . . . Not faces, not individuals, but an electromagnetism of attitudes linked and amplified and cohered out of the totality of root bipolar copulations . . . moved on by some great magnetic rhythm of repeated gestures.)

He looked around. These little and squat figures, self-sufficient in dark clothes . . . The continuity had been cut off and all elements were sequenced into a wrong procedural logic by these figures which remained purely of their ancient times.

Their first party. A big testing for them. He would emerge. . . . He had not changed his name yet. She, his wife, opposed it bitterly.

"I am what I am," she said.

"Yes, but a change in name—"

"No!"

"You changed it for mine once."

"No!"

He had not told her about Professor Biddle. Wives were out. If she became in some way not his wife . . . They had been arguing all day.

She was making canapés. She moved: short-limbed, her motions efficient, fitting perfectly into the small kitchen, her movements reduced to the absolute minimum. No ritual here and yet . . . ritual built around available space between table, stove, refrigerator, cabinets; her reflexes and automatic actions distorted by an inheritance from her mother (short and dark too, toughened through midnight flights and evasive courses throughout Europe), kitchen secrets out of place in an academic community, out of synch with modern times. Those movements excited him. Busy and unaware of a different kind of spying. She wore shimmering dark stockings; high heels; pearls draped on her collarbones; a simple sheath of black crepe (ultimate distillate of what the women around Targ wore). An Aphrodite of the kitchens, cool, redolent in her mystic motions of domesticity, yet evoking great controlled hungers and lusts.

(No, she no longer evoked the usual lusts. Not anymore. That sense came from a nervework that fed into him from the outside. He was changed and watched her as a stranger. He was part of something else now and not himself. Outside, there was a babble of voices not yet arrived, yet there. Being late, she was desperate and her motions were speeded up. He wanted to bust up the rhythm and periodicity of the motions in which she encapsulated herself (gestures of avoidance; warding off threats), motions that were reproachful, self-righteous, almost superstitious . . . motions which tempted him. Outside, "she" waited for a him not yet made, this other of these others, appearing to him as a someone, some kind of person he had learned to always have wanted. If only he fucked her, he would break her down and in.)

Lusts. He had leaned on the doorway—yes, that was it—watching her movements and then, suddenly, he had been overcome with desire. He had moved in, laughing but brutally purposeful, listening, watching his timing. If he began now, they would be here before he was finished. He had clasped her waist, kissed her neck through her hair. She laughed. "Stop." He pressed close against her, his penis rising against the feel of the top of her behind muscles, reaching and clasping her breasts, trying to fuse himself into her. But there was no room to lie down. "Stop"; she laughed. He heard a note in her laugh. Panic and lust: panic that she did not know who he was; lust that she knew who he was. "We have no time. They'll be here soon."

Good, he thought; just right.

(A babble of voices from some great background, past and future; present, pulsating, interweaving. A frieze. Mystery of the bas-relief . . . he understood it now; its relationship of figure to background field; field which was the potential to be any forms and faces and bodies and yet remaining itself. The logic and flow pattern of great fucking and exchange of sex-circuit towers erected by great civilizations. Once, in the ancient days (as in India), chisel-etched and integrated by hand, sign, mouth, instruction, cock, gesture, cunt, signal, caress, arsehold . . . passing, accelerating, and accreting great gouts of energy through each way station, whose circuitry was a coupling, changing through a recombination of elements which threw together into a Targ, a Helen, then subsided into background.)

He heard voices outside, knew they sensed, and the sensing excited him more; heard Targ's voice and heard his own voice, Trag's, saying, "Letum come." Their hips banged against the corners of cutting boards and refrigerators and against gas knobs. He turned her around. They kissed. She broke away. He reached for her and grabbed her. She was frightened now.

("You remember that time when . . ." he used to say to Helen.

"I don't." She always denied it.

"You don't want to remember."

"I don't remember, I tell you.")

And, as always, he had the sense that his wife was outside, watching as he pressed against her. She was long-legged. His penis pressed against the bottom of her buttocks. He turned her around. They kissed. Her left hand reached behind her to place a completed canapé on a large tray while the right grabbed his penis through his pants. She giggled and broke away. She unzipped his pants. She pulled out his penis with one hand. With the fingers of the other, scooped a dollop of pâté. She planted it on his penis. She bent to swallow it. Then rose to kiss him. He licked pâté from her lips. He bent suddenly,

(but all elements were sequenced into a wrong

procedural logic; logics that were incompatible. Peasant woman in black crepe, island man, Trag, wife, Targ, Helen. Kairos. Missing elements would have to be found and inserted into their proper places all over again. Somehow wife, Trag, peasant woman wearing pearl necklaces, and island man had disappeared from the sequence. Kairos. Bottom of the sequence simply not there. If he could only recover the ancient university wisdom of the sorting of the proper sequence, the mode of procedure, the universal algorithm ritual, he would understand now this sudden and inexplicable lust for these sexless island women.)

lifted her dress, pulled down her pants while she said, "Wait. They'll be coming soon. Wait for them." He put his hands on her behind, lifted her high, and planted her on his penis, one of his arms holding her, one of her arms holding him, and, turning and turning, they continued to make canapés.

"You remember that?" he used to say to his wife.

"I don't." She always denied it.

"You don't want to remember it. You've blocked it out."

"I don't remember."

Targ was through the town in a few minutes. The men hung together in idle clumps as they did all over the Mediterranean, looking as though they were in mystic conclave. They were really bored, mysterious with not doing (only a persistence of belief that a blank face concealed mystery instead of nothing at all made them intriguing). They stared at Targ as he passed and repassed; the children stopped playing and watched; the women paused for a second and then passed on. Then, since the light was almost gone and the cart-wide road faded a few steps in front of him, disappearing between stretches of waist-high grain, he turned back. There was no electricity on the island; a few oil lamps patch-lit the street. There was nothing to do, Targ decided, but to go back to the village café and get a drink. He thought he heard a few tinkly snatches of a tango being played, as on an old Victrola. He heard some radio static and thought it impossible that anyone could have a radio here. But as the sound soon faded, he decided it was something he hadn't really heard.

No sign announced it, but Targ could tell it was a café. The biggest crowd of men hung around as if judgment were handed out there, but it was only the boredom that drove them to these places. He had seen it in every small, hopeless Mediterranean town, in the mountains, at the seashore. Inside, a few men were sitting around a table drinking. A woman sat near the back of the room at another table. She was half in shadow, dark, almost black-skinned, black-haired. She wore black. Her black eyes were the only thing that looked alive about her, but not quite human because they passively caught and reflected the light from lamps the way an animal's eyes did. One window was open. It looked out over the sea. It was now night. The faceted lights of the mainland port twinkled in from far over the sea; they were festive and glittering as if a perpetual carnival were going on. The sea was glittered with the lights of pleasure boats and warboats passing. Targ thought it was going to be a long night. There was nothing to do but drink or go to bed. He tried to imagine that he was at a cocktail party. He addressed silent comments to the men and the woman as if they were to colleagues who talked to one another, speaking as people did at this hour, inane conversations all over the world. As he walked in, the men sensed his presence, apprehending him with receptors other than sight. Being from the outside, he had learned to sense being sensed, followed, tracked. By the time he was seated he had been fully examined.

Mr. Kairos stopped at the door. He stood there, pale, wearing a cap of silly summer tweed, holding his cane jauntily a third of the way down the shaft, against his narrow shoulder like a rifle. He looked younger. The night was behind Mr. Kairos; cricketlike insects, the faint sea surge, a dog's bark, a child's cry, the late-summer murmur of hoarse voices talking, all hung in the darkness. Lights glowed from fireflies and burning cigarettes. Mr. Kairos looked around; his eyes saw everything and nothing. The men didn't look his way, but their attention found him. Mr. Kairos saw Targ sitting and came in. He sat down at Targ's table. "Ahhh . . . it is still the same. Nothing ever changes here. That's the wonder of it. Probably it will never change. They don't know their terrific heritage. Perhaps Odysseus stopped here. Who knows? Not knowing their past prevents them from losing it by trying to rewrite it."

"When were you here last?" Targ asked him, to make conversation.

"Two thousand years ago." Kairos laughed. "Which is to say before the war. Nineteen thirty-nine. I was younger then; that is to say I was in a manner of speaking very young. These men might be the very same men who sat around that table and drank then and whom I drank against. They might never have even moved. How beautiful."

"Is that something to admire?"

"Once I would not have said it. I would have denied it vehemently, dear boy, but progress, if we can call it that, or ask, sir, what it even is, isn't everything."

"But stasis is?"

"I sometimes think that there should be no other state. But then I think of the unfortunate of the world who would be caught forever in that way . . . savage, half starving, verging on imbecility, superstitious . . . Still . . . Progress, industry, business . . . yes. On the other hand, stasis . . . It's a question of balances and points of comparison . . . referent points. The signs of 'the Beginning' should be, *must* be allowed to remain without alteration . . . and if altered, restored. Somewhere we went wrong."

"Why?"

"Isn't it obvious?"

"But what's restoration but what we make it? We try to solve the scale of events and development, fail or succeed without knowing it, and then, out of boredom, or under the compulsion of theory, we say: Here, this artifact fits precisely between this and that artifact, this birth here, this death there, this fucking along this line. Chains of being. Viconian-cycle chains. Strings and networks set along a critical path. Or what? Chaos? That's the way it goes. . . . And yet we arrive at chaos and correct what? The point, the theory-disruptive box of events that throws everything off in the future."

Curiously enough, Kairos nodded. They were silent.

They didn't say anything for a while. They were brought drinks. Targ drank quickly, and wondered how the hours were going to pass till morning. He hoped he would soon get sleepy, but he was too restless. An indefinable tension. Having nothing or no one to absorb it, it radiated back at him, bounced off the men, the women, the walls, the black night, and its reflection made him more restless.

Several times Mr. Kairos started to say something, but Targ kept his face blank, preoccupied; Mr. Kairos's tentative little throat clearings faded away to nothing. It would be pointless to go out, Targ thought. There was nowhere to go, nothing to see in the blackness. Targ thought of telling Mr. Kairos that progress could have enabled them to walk around in the night, but he didn't feel like getting into a long discussion about it. The men sat immobile, hunched over their drinks, not talking, no longer curious, but still not relaxed in the presence of strangers; and even though they appeared too far away to hear or, if they could hear, understand what Targ and Mr. Kairos might say, they seemed to listen. Targ looked for signs of rank, but couldn't find them.

The door opened and a uniformed man came in. He was tall, thin, slouch-shouldered. His visored cap was set low and squarely on his head, showing bits of too-long blond hair at the sides, which curled upward because of the pressure of the hat rim. He kept stiffening nervously, jerkily, as if to remind himself to stand straight, but always fell back into a slouch. When he turned, his head, neck, and shoulders turned as a unit. He was young and tried to set his face into the unaging representation of Authority, but the long configuration of his face, the high cheekbones, the thin, sensitive lips, the slanted eyes, the uncut hair made him look like a boy who had just invented symbolist poetry. He wore a khaki uniform with blackened brass buttons; epaulets covered the shoulder straps; numbers tarnished almost to extinction were attached to his collar tabs; one button of his tunic was pushed halfway through its buttonhole. His sleeve edges were frayed, as were the pants tips; the crease edges were doubled, which showed that someone had pressed the uniform badly . . . and that it didn't matter. He looked around, saw Targ and Mr. Kairos, and came over to their table. He made a small movement, like the beginning of a bow, stopped, slouched, stiffened again, and asked for their papers. He barely looked through them and gave them back. "Tourists?" he asked, pitching his voice to denote surprise at the stupidity of anyone's coming to this island. The pitch of his voice indicated that he was talking for the natives.

"In a manner of speaking," Mr. Kairos said. The policeman's eyebrows rose a little. "Amateur archaeologists . . . time travelers come to see the antiquities."

"Those are precious few," the officer told Mr. Kairos.

"Or a few precious ones." Mr. Kairos laughed.

"That is as it may be. I have never considered it."

"Will you join us?" Mr. Kairos asked, waving at a chair.

"I cannot," the officer said. "Though nothing ever happens, I must make my rounds. Those," he said, nodding toward the men, "will sit there and drink themselves almost to insensibility. Then they will get up. They will march. Through the night—three years and I will never know how they do it—up the street. Singing. They do it though almost rigid with drink. They come to their houses. They go in. They sleep. Tomorrow it will be as though they have never drunk. *That* is our excitement."

Then why not sit, Targ thought, and get another kind of rigidity?

"Two years ago we had a theft. I held an inquiry. The island council held their own inquiry, of course. They are very touchy. They pretend we are not here. Perhaps we are not," he said softly, almost romantically. "No one, of course, told me anything. A piece of amber; some stone they account precious; an amulet; something, I can't remember what, nothing that anyone dare wear, for it would be recognized as stolen. Finally they blamed the tourists. That it was the wrong season, that there are never tourists . . . or perhaps had been some years before, had nothing to do with their fantastic accusations. Oh, sometimes a pleasure boat manages somehow to stop here for a few hours to look at the animals. . . . If anything, it would be the tourist who is traditionally robbed. None of that had anything to do with their logic." The officer's sarcasm was too heavy; a young man's sarcasm, Targ thought, the kind he got from the elect just after they had discovered their election . . . sophomoric. "For this I went to the Fouché Academy."

"But if nothing ever happens, then will they start stealing if you sit with us for a while? I mean will there be a call for a crime wave?" Targ smiled.

"I have my duties," the officer said, turning his body a little and looking at Targ, getting the implications of Targ's tone and not liking them; he stood straight and authoritatively. "Enjoy your 'antiquities,' though, heaven knows, there is really only one."

"One?" said Kairos.

"Oh, yes . . . no, there was once a piece of pillar that lay in the fields of the northwest quadrant. That was just about the time I started my tour of duty. Three years. They have since removed it and pitched it into the sea. In order to cultivate the ground, you see. Of course, the harvest begins tomorrow; one could watch that. There are what our priest likes to call the rites of consecration . . . which means that they suffer the fool. The harvest itself . . ."

"But the other relics?" Mr. Kairos said. He was agitated.

"I know of no other relics."

"The temple."

"Oh, of course, that's still there. It's a little too big to move, even for these brutes," the officer said, raising his voice. They didn't stir, but Targ was sure they heard and marked the statement. They sat there rigidly; now and then one of them raised his clay mug to his lips and drank. The policeman raised his hand, half waving, half saluting, and went out.

They sat there for a while, sipping their drinks. Mr. Kairos dawdled over his one drink; Targ was on his second. He kept looking out the window at the lights of the port far across the sea. There was no light in the waters at all, no luminescence, as if the waters themselves had been removed. Mr. Kairos stood up. "Aren't you going to sleep? It's better to begin early, before it gets hot."

"Not yet. I don't need much sleep."

"Don't drink too much," Mr. Kairos said and laughed.

"Why not?" Targ asked him. He looked at Targ and his eyes were watery again, disappointed. The mustache drooped. The lower lip glistened. The shoulder shrugged. The mustache moved and Mr. Kairos was smiling sadly and that sadness annoyed Targ. Mr. Kairos turned and went; in the doorway he faded from a pale patch to a white glimmer down that corridor of blackness till absorbed by it.

The men continued to drink. There were four of them. Two sat quite close to one another, their thick shoulders almost touching. The other two sat at two angles, all to complete a triangle around the square table. The triangle of their position seemed to have no relationship to the square of the table, and yet he noticed there *was* a relationship though he couldn't figure it out. They all wore heavy blue shirts, faded around their armpits; shapeless hats, something like Phrygian caps; black canvas or corduroy pants. They sat hunched over the heavy tables, handling their handleless cylinders, drinking with violent, angular motions. They drank according to some sort of complicated procedure, a preconceived plan long worked out; that or they were involved in a contest in which innumerable, unclear, long-arranged handicaps were involved. They all made the same motion as they lifted the clay mugs to their lips; they set the cups down in the same way. Targ told himself he was seeing a genuine, living, still unspoiled folk ritual . . . sipping soma while they did the drunk dance with their hands. When they finished, one of them, the loser or perhaps the winner of the round (Targ couldn't be sure which), filled the cups from a stoneware bottle that was on the table. Every now and then the proprietor brought a new bottle.

Targ could hear the sounds of the breakers softened on the beach, but saw, again, nothing but the blackness and the port lights across the chasm. He drank again and again, but thought that the home-brew was as nothing to cocktails. The drink was only able to give his head a stuffed feeling. Padding pressed against the inside skin of his face and upward against the bone of his skull, mostly through the sinus of his cheeks and forehead, and a little through the nose (he still smelled salt water) and ears. Sounds were distanced, not so much distorted as diminished; and he realized he had stopped smelling the excremental stench hours ago. A vein began to throb over Targ's eye. He could feel the skin beside his lip twitch once in a while.

He discovered that he, in spatial relation to the others, constituted a fourth point, completing some kind of rhomboidal figure—or, was it pentagonal? As he drank more, his eyes played tricks, further reducing the men to beings less and less human and finally dissolving them to curves, planes, shadows, patches of light, receding or advancing according to the warmth or coldness of the color (and according to several dominant or recessive theories of art). Their faces were fractured by the uneven light. No one face was completely visible. Here a blade of light represented the side of a nose, a rough crescent that might have been a cheekbone shone, an irregular forehead patch, a skewed and bent rectangle that ran along the side of chins below lips, thin bow shapes of lower lips, boat shapes, eyes, two complementary triangles, but divided by a little gully of darkness . . . an upper lip . . . parts, parts gleamed. Targ's heart began to pound and the sense came that there was something he had forgotten and must know, or some act he had forgotten to commit. He shook his head to prevent the madness of gray from coming on him again. He tried to arrest the dissolution at this level, where it was merely amusing. He had to drink a little faster because their wretched grain brew couldn't get him drunk. Maybe if he got drunk enough, but not too drunk, he would understand the rules.

But the men responded to Targ. The tempo of their drinking increased and this made them seem human, complete again. Targ realized that somehow he had become a part of their contest. Perhaps they had lured him into it. Or he they. Or because the geometrical position had sucked him in. It was hard to tell. Their faces looked at Targ a little resentfully because he had broken their pattern, but at least they now acknowledged his existence, he thought, if only to hate him. Well, it was something to do, something to keep his mind amused, something to keep off the terror. Perhaps it was a running away, this wanting nothing more than to pass out, but he drank still faster. After a long while the peasants stopped suddenly. No order had been passed. There was no sign of any victory. They stood up. They were very drunk but very much in control of themselves. They didn't look at Targ. His sense of exhilaration passed. The contest was over. He heard the sound of many voices. The singing the policeman had spoken of? It didn't sound like singing.

Targ looked at his watch. It was still early and he was a long way from getting drunk; he was only a little high. He was afraid, now that the contest was over, the dissolution of everything into nothingness would start again. He was ready to run from it but there was nowhere to run and no Helen to run to or to come to him. Kairos? Ridiculous. He would run from it, but along a prevalence of force lines. He was perspiring. But she was there; the woman standing in front of him. Her black hair was parted in the middle; the part was very wide, its underlying skin shining. Her thick cheekbones stood out beyond her temple line, curving in till, passing her thick, her almost Negroid lips, they became heavy, smooth round jaw. She waited like some domestic animal. She was short. One of those women most of whose weight was concentrated in head, shoulders, breasts, and in the great hips. Her waist was almost inconsequential; her legs thin in comparison to the monumental shoulders. His first wife would have been like this when she got older. She had been quite slim but strong-boned. . . . She waited. And then Targ understood what it was he had won in the contest.

"Can I refuse?" Targ asked her. "Aside from your too great charm, can I hope to violate a custom, insult the mores of the land?" But he took care to speak in English. She didn't understand. She waited patiently, ready to offer up the product of her body: milk, food, sex, something she was overflowing and surplus with.

Targ stood up and walked out, leaving some money on the table. Though he didn't look back, he knew she was following. It was completely dark outside but the edges of the buildings were vaguely radiant. Targ found his way back to the inn. It amused him that he was drunk enough to abandon himself to something direction-finding in himself; he could never have done it sober. She came behind Targ. He walked up the stairs. He walked quietly along the corridor, tiptoeing, not wanting to wake Mr. Kairos. Mr. Kairos's door was open, a darker darkness in the blackness, a pit from which issued sighs and small bubbling snores. He didn't hear her step but she was behind Targ. She followed him into the room. He shut the door. He lit a match. He saw a candle stuck in a dish and lit that.

In the half darkness she removed her clothes. Her breasts were huge; the nipples and their areoles seemed to cover about a quarter of the breasts, which looked there in the flickering light substantial, black, unwavering. But her face, Targ now saw, was not smooth-skinned. She was pockmarked. There was a clear mark, a shininess of skin that slightly reflected the light, running from above her left eye all the way down her face, down the side of her neck, down the side of her breast, curving around under the breast as though cupping it, crossing over the swell of her belly, then down, following along the side of her belly where it narrowed, shooting inward suddenly to end on the great swell of flesh that held the pit of her navel. The hair of her pubes curled thickly up to halfway between her vagina and her navel, where it cut off suddenly as though shaved, bounded by a smooth, decisive line. The great thighs of her short legs were, Targ thought, interpreted by a sculptor who had tried to achieve the measured and curved graces of Greek lines but, having only a short distance in which to do it, had wrought violently in globular chunks, compromising somehow the smooth lines with abrupt muscle endings which started visibly through the olivy skin. Her calves were thick, swelling outward and downward, fading into the thick bone of the carefully incised ankle, those great muscle fibers clustering in and curving around the bowed tibia. "What a concept of art we might have had, had Phidias used you," Targ told her. She chose not to answer.

She lay down on the bed, no nonsense, none at all, spread her legs, knees up and out, and waited. The great fat clusters on the sides of her thighs spread outward, the breasts flattening to soft, thick disks, the belly not so humped now; the navel as in a jelly, oscillating softly for one or two shakes; she sighed and waited. Even that prostitute in Athens had cajoled a little, had made gestures of love, but civilization had not yet reached this far, Targ thought. As Targ undressed, he told her little words of love in several languages, any but her own, mocking her a little. Her eyes showed no curiosity at all. Targ tried Sanscrit, Lithuanian, Hebrew, and (the way he imagined it must have been spoken) the Indo-European word for "love." He stood by the side of the bed, naked. She merely waited; her eyes did not comment. Her impassive face revealed that there was no ur-word for the pretension of love in her lexicon . . . or that Mr. Kairos was probably wrong about these people. Targ sat down beside her and trailed his fingertips along the scar and up again. The flesh on either side of the blaze mark prickled. In spite of the appearance of glossy smoothness, the mark had the feel of something textured, like parchment, or cloth. She closed one eye. The lid of the other was held open by a pucker of scarred flesh. The eye rolled upward and looked above and behind toward the place where a headboard might once have been. That she was repulsive excited him and he thought: She is a three-eyed girl: two eyes for the day and one for the night. Targ thought he might call her Cyclops's daughter, or pretend he was enslaved by Cybele, peasant goddess of fecundity; it would make her more interesting. She smelled like sour wine, was a little older than he'd thought, and was scarred. But then he always made love in the comparative, or dialectical, mode. Helen there in the room: that excited him, as it once excited him to make love to his wife thinking of all the Helens.

But the more Targ stared, the more she seemed to dissolve into an agglomerate of fecund ellipses, practically a lesson in art perception, all except for the one eye, which turned away from Targ, out of politeness or boredom, peering away and above her. Targ bent down. He put his nose to her flesh. She smelled now, acrid sweat, the ubiquitous animal dung smell, the wine, sunlight, fish, rot, and loam. Targ wondered what she thought; she made no sound. Targ wondered what he thought. Targ bit her skin. It brought her to life again. Targ wondered if Helen, sleeping in Paris, dressed in her loneliness, silken and muscular, tasted, to anyone in particular, of meat and perhaps a little salt and certainly soap. Targ kissed Helen and mounted the woman. And feeling flesh now, but still as through a very thin piece of cloth, began to move in ancient and immemorial rhythms, accepting (though she would not respond) the night's second contest in joy. The strategy was to make her feel, to restore her, to break her down, in relation to her enjoyment, from something merely curved, planed, clothed, native, and mounted to a human being who would look at him, agonized or hating or loving, as Helen looked at him. And though she had fallen apart into abstractions, the unifying point of her existence was her flesh, her cunt, which was not abstract. Her open eye slowly, slowly began to lower, to no longer contemplate the darkness above her but look at Targ. What did she feel? What did she see? Did the act of passion lid her sight? Would it close? Targ went on like this for a long time, varying his sexual tempi, trying to work from the abstraction of the rhythms to some passion that would join the body underneath and him together. They kept looking at one another and soon, seeing he was still involved in the contest, he found a joy in this and desired only to close her eye, to make her show, by shutting it, that love was making her flesh involuntary. She, meshed with and moving against him, moaned, but the sound was nothing in the way of love; indeed, if you could interpret a moan (and how could you?), it seemed to be a response to something entirely different. And at last the staring eye angered him, that cool eye, and the anger made him pant. The bed shrieked, yes, and the floor groaned. He wondered if Professor Biddle—he meant Mr. Kairos—could hear them. He hoped so. And then the touch of passion reached her and the one wild eye turned round its circumference once. He tried to stop himself in order to frustrate her. He felt that his penis had begun to swell enormously, beyond control, and he tried to pull back but he couldn't. Something seemed to have mounted him. What rode his back? What had jammed up his arse and thrust him back and forth now? He couldn't turn to see what it was that possessed him. Was it Helen? He had a quick memory, something almost forgotten, blotted out, of many people now in the same dim room, all linked in some Eleusinian mystery (which was nothing more or less than groupfuck), but it had nothing to do with this. Was it Kairos? Had Kairos mounted Helen? Ridiculous. He was too old.

She yelled and her voice cracked a little. The terrific strength of will and muscles that held her heavy-cheeked face to impassivity flickered and she turned old, old, very old. He was fucking an ancient crone, almost bald, with one eye in the center of her head, and her long, almost tentaclelike breasts wove like blind pythons, tongue-nippling at his face, his eyes, burrowing into his ears. Targ tried to shy away but he was held, encapsuled there by old bones and skinny, gnarled, knot-muscled legs. Her wrinkles were themselves finely muscled, like tendrils clutching, and his hands, which held her arse, gripped down to bone, and crone fingers pecked into his shoulders and arse. The excitement was almost enough to make Targ feel himself getting intolerably excited, but he passed out first without coming and felt, as he fainted, he had won and preserved himself.

4

Targ woke, stretched, and knew she wouldn't be there even before he felt she had left. She was gone. They always left. It was traditional. Did they go because they feared to see the look on any Targ's face when he woke and saw them? In that case, what look, fair lady? Targ thought. No revulsion different than the ordinary kind for everyday things. Or did they go in order to spare all Targs the horror of having to make that face? This act in turn aroused the feelings that the face represented. In which case, no need, Targ thought. *This* Targ slept with it; he woke with it; alone or with someone else he always had it, that face. Or were men, in terminating their piggish, postcoital sleeps, required to show this disgust? A mask. It was traditional to be gone. Targ stood up. The pitcher of water on the carved chest of drawers was full, but it was too much trouble to wash.

Targ looked out the window. The sun was fairly high. His watch had stopped and he wasn't sure of the time: no bells announced the change of classes or work shift and the Mediterranean sunlight here was permissive, decadent, undecisive, untimed. He was on his own. He saw the beach, shining metallically, polished evenly by the morning sun. The land rose away from its shiny rind, green, domed into succulent fruitfulness. Domed? Yes, that was it. *Domed.* What a peculiar geological formation. Domed. The sea was hard and blue under the morning light; its rough wave edges were burnished into permanent silver. Of course Targ thought: "samite-sheeted; the trackless waste, the wine-dark sea," trapped by words which, in turn, tarnished this sea with a traditional modifier and made it trite. (He made a discovery. It had never been trite to those men who first modified reality with those first words. He made a second discovery: that those had been poets and it was the word alone that mattered, not the sea . . . and that the word itself barely even expressed their own feelings.) Far out over the water a little white smudge shone; that would be the port, still looking as if it were lit up. Targ put on clean underwear, a pair of denim jeans, a white shirt with a button-down collar, and a pair of blue deck shoes (no socks), and went out.

But the door to Mr. Kairos's room was still open. He was already dressed, sitting on his neatly made bed, apparently waiting for Targ. His legs were crossed and his long body was bent over, crumpling the shiny whiteness of his suit, a little as if he was in pain. The great, knobby hands were folded over the head of his cane, but showed between his barred fingers the leering gargoyle head and a cigarette. Resting, his chin was compressed and the ragged tips of his mustache brushed the mottled skin of the backs of his hands. He saw Targ and his eyebrows rose, as though mocking. Mr. Kairos wished to say something serious; he was troubled so his expression of cynicism and conviviality was inappropriate. How long would Targ have to wait, he wondered, before Mr. Kairos said something admonishing like "Targ, I want you to know that Helen is a wonderful girl and . . ."?

"I know," Targ said. "No one knows it better than I."

But misunderstanding this answer to a whole series of optional questions, choosing the wrong unspoken question, reading it as apology for tardiness, Mr. Kairos mockingly said, "Sleep knits up the raveled sleeve . . ." the sense of quoting being strong and coy in his tone. Mr. Kairos straightened up, uncrossed his legs, and laughed while managing to look mournful.

"But time persists in unraveling: Penelope," Targ said. He felt physically good; she had not drained his excess of energy after all. He had slept long and well.

"You have missed so much of it. . . ."

Targ had been all over the world; Targ had read all of history; he had studied all the customs: therefore, what had he missed?

". . . the rising at dawn, the invocation, the procession, the consecration, the sacred dances . . ."

From Frazer on, or from Herodotus back, what had Targ missed? Lévi-Strauss, Malinowski, Mead and Firth, Morgan, Durkheim . . . What had he missed? Only he now remembered little or none of it. "I thought I dreamed thunder, but I needed my sleep," Targ said.

"Regard the ant," Mr. Kairos said and stood up.

"Is this some kind of holy day?"

"No, not exactly. There is no festival today, no celebration appears on the calendar of the Church. But in the island's hagiography it is most important: a day of obligation. The harvest begins today."

What was there to harvest? Targ wondered: all that vegetation, indiscriminate and green, or brown, depending on the crop. And all crops like another, to become bread then flesh. "Rye, pumpernickel, gluten, whole wheat, white, millet, what?" Targ asked. Mr. Kairos laughed, stood up, and linked his arm in Targ's, and they crabbed out the door together and went down the stairs. Had Targ ever *seen* a harvesting? Kairos wondered.

Certainly. Egyptian hieroglyphics; harvest scenes on Greek vases; "The Angelus," Breughel, "The Solitary Reaper," "The Man with the Hoe." There were those neat *Life* and *Fortune* and Sunday-supplement sections, photographs of threshing machines moving along an endless Kansas (presumably Kansas, but Targ wasn't sure; he could ask the geography, economics, or agriculture department) sweep. He had, Targ decided, seen many harvests after all, but he just couldn't remember them.

They went downstairs. Mr. Kairos had already found out that they didn't serve meals at the inn, but they could get something to eat at the café; there was no other place on the island. Targ wondered if she would be back there, staring equally out of both eyes, equably at him, having reduced him to a man among the men whom she serviced . . . a statistic. There were no men in the streets, no women, only some small children playing. Their shouts were sharp, cold enough to cut through the warm air. The building walls shone pink, gray, and white in patches; the washed-out red of the gabled roof rims hung over the street. They could see the road, white, too narrow for automobiles, straight and simple, going up to the top of the island, where, perching above it all, only its roof seen, was the little temple.

Mr. Kairos kept babbling: ". . . and they pray on the harvest morning for a good harvest, for no mischance; they offer to the Virgin and, of course, for her son. Naturally they must be careful about the prayers, omit nothing in the sequence, make no mistake, no stumbles, no stammers, or there would be bad luck. Vestiges of ceremonies to Ceres persist. Poor soil has made them fearfully superstitious. Africa is being moved northward, they say, pushing the wind before it. Their task is to have the great drought bypass them. Of course, great climatical changes *are* taking place. Perhaps the ice age is still receding and where jungle was, first plains and then desert come. Having been planted and harvested for thousands of years, the soil is so poor here everything takes a little longer to ripen. They must plant earlier, grow longer, and so rush to finish the harvest before the rain winds come sweeping up and ruin everything with their wind-forced wetness, dropping their intense loads of damp, then moving on, dry, to sear southern Europe. So heavy is the precipitation that everything mildews, rusts, molds with surprising speed. Mistral, sirocco, laveche . . . they have their own bitter name for it here. And so they must finish quickly. As it is they always finish the ingathering only a day or so before, sometimes even on the same day that the wind comes. So one can understand that they live on the edge of disaster all their lives . . . for centuries."

"Why don't they start even earlier?"

"They can only plant just so early. They must wait for the crops to ripen. Sometimes they have to reap unripened grain."

They came to the café, went in, and sat at a table. The owner made breakfast for them. There were no men here; apparently they were all harvesting. Targ had bitter coffee—chicory and grain water, really—nothing else. Mr. Kairos had some rough peasant bread and a spread, some grease, an omelet with canned meat in it, and a little wine. He kept talking about the crops, going into it thoroughly, looking at Targ now and then disapprovingly as though to ask why he didn't seem more interested. Mr. Kairos gave it all: statistics, mores, customs, modes, the delicate ecology. ". . . but you see, they are really completely independent of imports and have nothing worth exporting. Grain in summer; fish in winter. Wine. Some olives. Life is hard."

"If life is hard they should inherit the world . . . or come to nothing," Targ said, sipping. "Where did you get all this?" Targ asked; he smoked a cigarette.

"I had a talk with the priest after the ceremony. He reminded me that I could still remember a bit about it from the last time I was here. But it's all in the brochure," Mr. Kairos said.

Peculiar construction. "The priest?"

She hadn't come. She probably came only at night. That was traditional too. . . . Of course she wouldn't; not during the harvest.

What would Mr. Kairos think if he turned, left, hunted her down, and spent the rest of the day in bed with her? He would admonish Targ. "I think that Helen is too fine . . ."

When Mr. Kairos had eaten, they went out into the sunlight. As they passed, the children stopped playing, stared at them; and began again when they had gone. They passed the police station. Next to it was the last building in town, the church. It was square, simple, having only two undecorated windows, which flanked the wooden door. Only the flaked gilt cross on top announced that it was a church. The building was white on top, fading to yellow downward. There were dark smudges like smoke stains at the bottom, radiating upward.

"Oh, yes, there's an interesting history to those marks. One year the crops came in a little too late; or the winds came too soon. The crops failed. They grew outraged and attacked the church and the statues for having been so bad to them; they even attacked the Jesus . . . they take their relations with God personally. Having made their prayers properly, they felt that the least the Lord might have done was to reciprocate. They burned the crucifix. They also killed the priest."

"The church withstood it."

"Well, after all, the building is said to go back to Charlemagne. They built well in those days. The walls are six feet thick."

"Charlemagne?"

"Yes; at that time the Franks tried to use the island as a base for attacking the infidels."

"But . . ."

Kairos shrugged. "They were driven off the island. Then the Mohammedans tried to cover their flank and were also driven off. There is a legend that *this* was the place, actually, in which Roland and Oliver met their end."

Philidor would be interested, but it wouldn't change his mind. He would say that the world was not ready to have its illusions shattered.

"At any rate, they tried to save the crops from the damp, but it rotted at an astonishing rate. When they were about three-quarters finished with the harvesting, they saw it would not be good. That's the margin they live on."

"It sounds as if they could use some of those miracle grains."

"Yes. Yes. That's it. Of course. It would be perfect," Kairos said, very excitedly. "Then they could save, store up, and such tragedies needn't happen."

"Tragedies?"

"They came raging in out of the fields; the men, the women, even the children. They had torches." And Mr. Kairos dramatized it, seeming almost to dance it, sprightly with outrage in spite of his age, brandishing his cane, holding it by its tip while the polished head flickered in the sunlight, shooting off flames from the polish on the leering eyes and twisted mouth.

"It's a bad building," said Targ. "Too cubical."

"But simple. Very early Christian," Mr. Kairos said. "Dignified." And he lunged downward and buried the head of his cane in the grass that ran around the edge of the church, as if it were a torch. He stepped back as if looking at his work. His mouth was open in an unvoiced "Aaaaaahhhh," as if seeing the flames rise; his Adam's apple bobbed as he enjoyed the remembered burning with a senile delight.

"It sounds almost as though you were here."

"Oh, I was. Thousands of years ago. Many times. I was here. At least in my mind. Or in dreams. You know how dreams are . . . like reality . . . realer, and when you've dreamed dreams it's like an experience you can never forget. In fact . . ." And Mr. Kairos's eyebrows went up and his eyes became unfocused as if remembering. His mouth made motions, chewing on some shred of memory. They passed a little cemetery. It ran long, thin, compressed against the roadside for a quarter of a mile. But there were only a few grave markers there, most of it empty. The fields began as soon as the town ended; in fact, beneath the house windows that looked inland. They swept up without apparent boundary or property markers. As they walked up, they could see the natives, far off to the left, harvesting. The sun was hotter here in the fields; hot green and grain smelled good. The road was dusty and narrow, almost a path.

"Of course, there are no automobiles here, so they don't need wide roads. Besides, where would they get gas?" Halfway up the hill they paused and Mr. Kairos walked down a little path that branched off to circle the island at that level. He walked for twenty paces along the path and stopped. "There used to be a few marble blocks here, something preclassical, a pedestal base, I think, but it doesn't seem to be here anymore." Mr. Kairos's face was caught in some muscular spasm which made parts of it shake, twitch, as he, agitated, pointed his quivering stick to where the shrine, or whatever it was, was supposed to be. The stick pointed to a slight, even depression where the grain tops had not grown as high as the rest of the field.

"But the officer said they took it away," Targ told him.

"But a shrine. Of such antiquity. Paleolithic."

"Stones to them. What does antiquity mean? Stones. Memory," Targ told Mr. Kairos and felt wild satisfaction that his saying "stones" that way disturbed Mr. Kairos. Let him, Targ thought, learn what I have unlearned; he's never too old.

"The rocks were hewn so roughly."

"That much space might make a loaf of bread."

"I hope they haven't done that to everything."

"No," Targ told him, pointing. "See: the temple's still there."

They got to it after an hour's ascent. It didn't look like its picture at all. It was pocked by the action of the winds, flaked by damps and heat, but still, in the sun's hard sheen, it seemed plastic-coated. Seen from certain angles, it was perversely modernistic, a debased caricature of Greco-Roman. Close up it wasn't even white, but shades of gray with black scars; all droppings-stained. One of the pillars had tumbled down, but was rolled back, close to the temple, away from any available growing ground. The grain grew right up to the edge of the temple. Mr. Kairos sat down on one of the tumbled pillarstocks and sighed. It all looked shabby and unimportant.

"I thought you were here before?" Targ asked him.

"I was. I don't remember it looking like this."

"A few years have aged it. Or after all, thousands of years, you said."

Mr. Kairos looked at Targ seriously. "No. Not thousands. That's just my little joke. A little more than thirty. Sometime just before the war."

"Well, that *was* thousands of years ago."

Kairos looked puzzled.

"Morally, if not chronologically." Still, Targ thought, he didn't get the same panicky feeling he had had at the Parthenon. Perhaps because it *wasn't* the Parthenon; because it wasn't *supposed* to be superb: *the fount.* "But let us pretend that this is older than old. A real find."

Mr. Kairos kept shaking his head, mourning; his sad eyes looked everywhere and nowhere. Targ was annoyed at his distress: what was there to be sad about? A few chiseled stones; no more.

"Let's pretend that it is the last relic of a lost race."

"It is a small temple and was perfect in its way."

"Yes, a remnant of the age of gold: Atlantis itself," Targ told him. A few swallows shot out from underneath the overhanging pitted acanthus leaves and whipped off into the sky, twittering. "Age enhances perfection," Targ told him. "I don't have to tell you that, Mr. Kairos. So this is fit to be a companion, if not the duplicate, of let us say Nike Apteros."

From there they could see the whole island. It was almost perfectly circular, having no bays or inlets. Around it, the smoothness of the sea was broken by skirmish lines of pleasure boats. Beyond, along the way they had come, the mainland was misty enough to be taken for a cloud, or the smoke of a world on fire. A bird, somewhere in the high grain, sang three bell-clear notes and warbled wildly up, high into the range of inaudibility. A dog's faint bark drifted slowly up like smoke. They could hear goat sounds quavering in the pleasant heat. The sun was warm and the marble stored the warming. The wind was announced by the sight of a soft rustle of grain; it blew, bringing the sun-warmed smells of sea and freshly cut grain. Insects buzzed softly, steadily; they flickered in and out of visibility in the sun-heated air waves. High above the temple, the little flight of birds wheeled wildly back and forth before plunging like pursuit planes suddenly, shooting down the green flank of the hill toward the town. Higher, gulls circled, the wheel of them drifting from one side of the island to the other, and out to sea. Still higher, silver pinheads of light trailed vapor festoons. Only Mr. Kairos's face, child-twisted with disappointment, was sad in this place. He looked at the temple as though he had come too late; something had been missed. He shook his head to see the damage, as though the slow flaking, the decomposition, the weather stains, the careless desecration of the birds, all, had been done by vandals, not nature, all between the time they had looked at the photograph and now. "If only we had left earlier for the island."

"Appearing this way bespeaks a greater antiquity," Targ comforted, but it only seemed to hurt Kairos. "I mean what's antiquity? A conventionalized sequence fixed by an investment of passionate belief. After all, carbon dating's been proved a wrong tracking device. Everything is in flux. All standards collapse. *Continents* turn out to be peripatetic, not philosophers. New kinds of stars are discovered every day. Nuclear particles and motions proliferate hourly. Space is left- or right-handed. *Strangeness* is a movement. And what's parity but what seventeen obdurate men dominating a conference of scientists, monetarists, or agrarians decide? The Creation, or the Grand Reordering by the Demiurge, lies in the future, depending on a Red Alert. . . . See how it trails above us?" The speech exhausted him.

Mr. Kairos's shoulder dropped away; his suit was getting soiled fast. Targ was annoyed that Mr. Kairos had been stupid enough to wear white. "You shouldn't mock," Mr. Kairos told him.

"Why not? What else is there?"

"You're still young . . . you're married. You shouldn't think that way."

And Targ waited for him to say, "I'm fond of Helen; I think you married a wonderful girl. Argive Helen." Targ was ready for him.

"Great tasks lie before you."

"I'm forty. I'm old." But seeing Kairos's misery, Targ relented a little. "Perhaps you are confusing it with something else you saw somewhere else?"

"No!"

"After all, thousands of years . . . a long time."

"That was my little joke. *Thirty* . . . a little more than thirty," Mr. Kairos said primly as though impressing a lesson on the willfully stupid young. "I tell you . . . But the photograph: what about that?"

"They are clever at these things."

"I don't believe it."

"Then perhaps it is merely that the natives are taking it apart and bringing it to the sea."

"Merely!"

"As an offering," Targ told him. "Or perhaps they are starting a new diocese. Or even, as they cast out some offending body, a node of infection, they renew their ancient war with their invaders. Or maybe they merely need more growing space."

Kairos was quite cast down. He half turned toward the temple and then away. He turned back, took half a step, stopped, turned away, shuffled a few feet down the hill. His mouth opened, closed, opened, closed.

"Aren't you going in?"

"I'm afraid," Kairos said.

"Why?"

"It will not be as it was."

"So?"

"I couldn't bear it."

"You're probably right. Let's go."

"No."

"Then let's go in."

"I couldn't bear it."

"Maybe it's the same."

"It isn't," said Kairos.

"It might be."

"I'm old. How many shocks can an old heart bear?"

"All right then, let's leave."

"Aren't you at all curious?"

"Not really."

"If I could describe the wonder of the way it was . . ."

"Yes."

". . . I would arouse your burning interest."

"No doubt."

"You doubt."

"I doubt." And then Targ saw what it was Kairos wanted. "All right. I'll go in and look and tell you if it's what it was."

"Look carefully."

And Targ went up the two steps and into the temple. It was cool, dim, damp, and gray inside. The brightness and the soft, salt-tanged heat outside, were like a wall of light which, even though there was no hidden inner room, no sanctuary, shut off the inside effectively. The cracked, eroded floor had some twigs on it, a little dirt, a few dried leaves; moss grew on the pillars. There was an almost empty little platform in the center which might have been an altar or have held some figure of an awful goddess: something to do with fertility; these temples always did. There was a bone on it. Targ picked it up. It had many scratches on it. He put it down. An ancient crusted device of gears lay beside the bone. It looked like part of some machine. He tried to move the gears. They gave a little, the merest fraction of an inch, perhaps a millimeter. He heard winds howl. Voices. Peripherally, he caught a faint motion on his wrist as if his watch dials were spinning, but when he looked directly they were still. He put the gears down. Something about the bone bothered him. He looked at it again. He picked it up and looked closely. The scratches were evenly spaced, as if they were calibrations. Above them were scratched circles and crescents, some bigger than others. He ran his fingernails over the scratches: a ratchet sound. When he got to the end of the bone, the air had changed, but he couldn't say how. It was . . . fresher. He moved his fingernail back, but not all the way because the sound made his spine shiver. The space under the roof was dark. Targ could see faint movings there, but not when he looked directly. Birds, Targ thought, leaving aftersights which grooved the darkness. "Come in," Targ called. Mr. Kairos didn't answer. Targ could see something which looked hard, small, brilliant, like some geometric figure, a crystal, moving out there, as though embedded in the general brightness. He went out. "Why didn't you come in?" Targ asked. "I called."

"You were in there a very long time."

"Only a few minutes."

"What did you see? What happened?"

"Nothing. Why didn't you come in when I called?"

"I didn't hear you. Nothing?"

"Nothing."

"You're sure?"

"Yes."

"Were there no statues?"

"No statues. Those are probably in Paris, or London or Athens, or New York. I saw some bones, a wheel or part of a gear box from some engine. . . . Why don't you go in and look for yourself?"

"Let's leave."

"But don't you want to see it?"

Mr. Kairos turned away.

"And after you've brought me all the way out here, in the middle of nowhere, to this dull blessed island, you won't even see the main attraction?"

"I'm terribly sorry . . ." Mr. Kairos began.

"I don't understand you," Targ said. "Well, there's nothing to see anyway. Don't bother."

"Of course you're right. I'll go in." Mr. Kairos started to turn back and walk up the stairs. But Targ couldn't stop himself; he stepped down, barred Mr. Kairos's way, took his arms, turned him around. "But I *will* go," Mr. Kairos said, trying to pull loose. The old man's feeble pull made the younger man's grip tighten viciously; the grip irreverently asserted itself and held tighter. Targ felt good, almost as though Mr. Kairos's old and tyrannous bones were about to snap like fragile crystal, chipping, cracking, each fracture striking off dissonant tones.

"Too late," Targ said. "You've missed your chance."

"But . . ." And Mr. Kairos kept trying to pull loose. ". . . you don't understand."

"Now it is forbidden. Closing time, you see. You've come too late," Targ said, finally feeling he had accomplished a wild desecration, something he hadn't been able to accomplish at the university or do to Helen. Targ began to laugh at Mr. Kairos's foolish and spluttering face. As though he had any dignity left, as though he still had dominion over me, Targ thought scornfully.

"Ahh, dear boy, you're joking, aren't you?" Mr. Kairos said and smiled. But when he turned and tried to go up the steps again, Targ held him for a second, even pulled him back. Mr. Kairos began to tremble, so Targ let him loose.

"Go then," Targ said. "See a votive offering of bird shit."

But instead they left, walking around the temple.

Behind the temple the road became a narrow but well-walked path. It went straight down till it ran out, far below, on the narrow beach. They passed a few houses set right against the path. They were crude, built out of pinkened, sun-hardened clay. Some children played in front of them, darting in and out of farmyard debris. There were no other roads except for a few neat and narrow paths that radiated out from the main road and circled the island. After a while

Mr. Kairos turned off and walked down one of the paths; Targ followed him. They walked, brushing against the grain, until Mr. Kairos's suit was almost completely covered with kernels of it. Once, passing some spot where the grain grew sparsely, Mr. Kairos said, "There was something here too."

"Are you sure? I see nothing. Whatever it was, it seems to have poisoned the ground."

"I'm very sure. They've taken it away."

"What was it?"

"A statue. It may have come from the temple."

"Art gives way to utility," Targ said.

"It wasn't a very good statue . . ."

"Then utility becomes artistic comment . . ."

". . . and it had been terribly eroded, lying out in the open that way, all these centuries. Probably an Apollo or a Zeus."

". . . as well as clearing up the debris and rubbish of the ages."

"But still, it had a certain majesty."

"Ozymandias?"

"No. The statue was religious; I'm sure of that."

Targ turned to look at the expression on Mr. Kairos's face. The eyes were mournful, serious. Targ laughed.

"You're laughing again," Mr. Kairos said sadly.

Targ couldn't stop; he felt better than he had in a long time. He plucked a blade of grain and chewed the stalk as they continued to walk.

Mr. Kairos looked at his watch. "It's late. There's nothing else to see except the harvesting."

"We'll be stuck here till tomorrow," Targ said. The sun beat on Targ's face and he could see little new clouds coming innocently up from the south in soft white festive spurts.

"I suppose you think it's a mistake, our coming here?" Mr. Kairos asked.

Targ shrugged.

"It *is* a mistake," Mr. Kairos said; but Targ didn't believe him.

"It doesn't matter."

"But there's nothing to do," Mr. Kairos admitted.

"We'll find something. Here as well as anywhere else," Targ told him.

They were approaching the harvesters, who were working in a great warped line up toward the east. They were all naked to the waist, the men and the women. They would cut up the long hill till they reached the top and then they would cut their way to the bottom of the island. Behind the line, thirty feet or so, stood people who directed them by beating rhythms on drums, sing-shouting. Targ couldn't understand the language. The palm beat was predictable; the finger tappings seemed completely unrhythmic, random. Together the variations were intricate and coherent; but the basic beat commanded unchangingly beneath the diverting patterns. Men—it couldn't be called singing—sounded; women replied. It was less song than conversation, more conversation than song: combination of group and individual voices in a sound mosaic of incredible richness . . . and yet, when they came close to the reapers, something was altered and the rhythms became more orderly, more predictable, duller. Had Targ heard the richness or imagined it?

Their bodies bent as they grasped the sheaves of grain with their right hands and swung their sickles to the accent of the drumbeat. They cut, followed through in their momentum to turn their heads and shoulders—swinging and swiveling still farther till they seemed almost about to launch themselves off their wide-set feet—ending up peering anxiously over their shoulders at the sky behind them. Their sickle tips pointed, all, simultaneously to the sky. They cut in even sweeps, their arcs overlapping intricately. They missed no spot. Behind, a second line bound up the grain into sheaves. Their faces were brown-glazed by labor sweat, sun, windburn, living, aging, and repetition. Only their dark eyes showed expression as they glanced behind them. But there was nothing to see but the rind of beach below, the flatness of the southwestern sea, lit in the slanting rays of the afternoon sunlight, and the light-brushed little clouds that cut through the sunny air. Four jet streams boxed a cloud.

"They rush against the wet wind. In this island they claim they can see him hovering, wet and wild, in the distance, slowly coming their way, before any clouds are even seen. They must harvest and gather before he gets here," Mr. Kairos said.

There he goes, Targ thought, thinking romantic thoughts.

Targ looked where the harvesters looked. There was nothing to the west or the south at all; only bird-filled air and boat-filled sea receding to the Spanish and African coasts a few hundred miles off. "And when the harvest is in?"

"They celebrate for three or four days; and that is a wonderful thing to see. Then life begins again. Then they go out and fish the waters in winter."

"No rest?"

"They cannot forgo the cultivation of the grain, the harvesting of the sea. They are a proud people. To miss a year would bring them to the verge of starvation. But rather that than a moral decimation."

"Of course, superstition . . ."

Mr. Kairos started to interrupt.

"Tradition, then, binds them more tightly, pointlessly."

"I admit that if there were a disaster they *could* get food from the mainland," Mr. Kairos said.

"Exactly."

"But to accept means that they must accept other things. Possible restrictions. Changes in their ways. Fertilizer, perhaps. A tractor or two."

"What is more restricted than this?"

"To them it is freedom. *They* choose their destiny."

"The destiny of ants."

"Dignity. Dignity, sir," Mr. Kairos told him.

"Maybe dignity is the ability to choose not being dignified." Targ smiled. "I don't see why they don't accept help. Everyone's doing it. What's the point of an existence like this?"

"In its way it is a full, therefore a rich life. They know nothing of the world. The currents of history have rippled to their shore, left their little marks in the sands of their existence, but have been mostly obliterated by the next wave, by the winds of time, by their very indifference. They go on," Mr. Kairos sang.

"But they work so hard . . . like animals," Targ said. He thought of the black liquid eye of Cyclops' daughter, staring with a debased sex worker's comprehension, no more. He thought of Helen's eye, capable of expressing so much more than mere comprehension: compassion, progress, self-denial, intricate variation, sexual combination, deferred orgasm. All right, Targ admitted. Hating her, I love her; did that answer Mr. Kairos's unspoken question?

Mr. Kairos inhaled deeply. The air, the hot sun, the smell of the crushed grain, the birds hovering or darting, the late butterflies ornamenting the grasses, the insects hopping away from the falling grain, the hiss—like wind—of the sickle swings, the constant rustle of the grain . . . All of it moved Mr. Kairos very much. "Here is certainty," his voice, now strong, said. "Look at them. Look at them!" And his voice rose again, pitched high into an almost soprano against the deep chant of the pacesetters and the flat, unmelodious beat of the drum. He pointed with the laughing head of his cane. "They reap." And his voice was enthusiastic, rising a little higher than the singing whistle of the swinging sickles as they swished and made their way slowly up the hill. The reapers didn't look at them at all; they hadn't been looked at since they had come. Only the pacesetters had glanced quickly at them and then looked back at the reapers' work. "Their motions are a dance that sprung into being in the most ancient of times. Each movement has an old and mystic meaning, stylized, perfect, the significance of which is long forgotten by the people themselves. But by some instinct, perhaps transmitted through inheritance, perhaps a wisdom handed down through the sexual act itself, they are compelled to dance the joyous dance that cuts the grain. Consider. They cut and bind in a line, all people beginning at the same time. Isn't that miraculous?"

"What's miraculous?"

"By the time they come to the middle, their line bisects the island exactly like a diameter."

"So?"

"But at the beginning, if they all begin at once, what must the shape of that line be?"

"A straight line?"

"No. No. It can't be. They, all bunched along some edge of the circumference, must begin in some miraculously convoluted and even self-crossing line, so complicated as to look disorderly, moving so that it gradually straightens itself out to a diameter and then begins its compressions and convolutions again, so that they finish like they began, all together."

It was more like a machine, Targ thought; they were like parts, each fulfilling its function, each at the mercy of some expedient, brainless, mathematical purpose that drove them. The insects rasped; the birds creaked; the drums clattered and rattled them up the hill: rhythmic, inexorable, harsh, and unoiled, shaking the earth as they came. For what? They existed in order to exist.

"And more: the diameter, the number of harvesters required to bisect the island, determines the relationship of the population to the land. How wonderful," Mr. Kairos said, "it would be to live here. How sweet to belong." He turned to Targ. His face longed. His mouth was open. His comic eyebrows were raised and his eyes were screwed into the pitiful attitude of want; his hand went out a little toward Targ; his cane, in the other hand, drooped down now. "Are you sure there was nothing else, that nothing else happened in the temple when you were in there?"

"Why?" Targ asked. He wished there were a stone to sit on. The reapers had worked their way closer. Targ suddenly had the impression that the reapers wouldn't stop but go right over them. They had to move back up the narrow path a little, about fifty feet away from the reapers. Being higher, they could see the whole line moving slowly upward, leaving the ravaged stubble behind. "What would you do here? You're too old to do that kind of work. There is nothing to do at night. I don't think there's a book to read on the whole island." He ignored the other question.

"I've read enough books. I might give back what I've taken in. Teach history . . . tell stories. They have no history, only legends."

"You can't even talk their language. Who would you talk to? The officer? The priest? *They* come from the same world you do."

"But to belong is to be as they are."

Machine parts, Targ thought. "And doing what? Planting, tending, reaping, fishing, and then the whole thing repeated again. You're too old for that; and even if you weren't, what kind of life is it?"

"It would be sweet to belong here, to live out one's life and . . ."

Mr. Kairos's stubbornness annoyed Targ. "What difference does that make?" Mr. Kairos could only see the romanticism of the place. Mr. Kairos had that silly, that comic notion that peasants were the happiest of people, living the richest of lives. In books they did; according to romantic poets and Christians they did, thought Targ. But even the view here was monotonous; this island too regular, this season too much on time. The life consisted of mere struggle to feed, to eke out of that bad soil those sad crops. Nothing at all, Targ had to admit, like the lush fields of grain one saw in the Sunday-supplement sections of newspapers at home, nothing like Kansas. And all of it dependent on disastrous chance.

"It gives life meaning," Mr. Kairos said.

"Does it?"

"See here: what's the matter, Targ?"

Targ was bored. Mr. Kairos had no right to ask him such a question in such a voice. You're dead, Targ thought, we're dead, everyone's dead: let us feel some life. Was the choice between overcivilized ghosts or somnambulistic machine parts? He slapped at a fly that bit suddenly and too hard. The rise and fall of civilizations, Targ thought at Mr. Kairos, is nonsense, insubstantiality, a simulations vision created and played out by the great poets–systems analysts, who cannot stand disorder and must find reason, structure, and sequence for everything . . . especially since the world did not conform to their expectations and their science. Therefore this place will go. The fly escaped the slap, rose, buzzed, and came shining through the air to light on the back of Targ's hand. I am bored, do you understand that, you old fart? Targ thought, and shook his hand violently. There is no reality. . . . When we're about to be destroyed . . . well, everything that has happened before becomes as nothing in the face of that. And he shook his hand violently two or three times before the fly fell loose; there was a tiny blood spot on the raised tendons of his hand.

"Is there something wrong between you and Helen? It's that, isn't it, Targ? She's a wonderful woman. . . ."

And what do we have now, Targ thought, and kicked, swinging his feet in step through the grain, scattering granules, but a handful of tyrannous, logical forms and bloody dust or flesh-mortar which must bind them together; myths in a million overbearing disguises. Yes. She *was* wonderful, but not a woman in the usual sense of the word at all. But from Ur to Harvard, it is all the same now, or becoming the same. There is nothing but the searing vapor, for we will *all*—not one, or this one, but *all*—be nothing tomorrow other than particles. So it makes it as if nothing is real, not Helen or her acting pained over me. Did the old fart understand that? Go ahead, he thought, and conjugate Targ a civilization, raise it and decline it through stages, and tell him it was birthed out of an inexorable law of nature. The play of muscles in Helen's arm, or the stare of Cyclops' daughter's lewd eye, or your droolings about the unspoiled, romantic meaning of what are a machine of flesh . . . "It's nothing," Targ said.

The sheen of the sun on the rank of bronzed backs; the consonant flash of sunrays on the sickles; a line of sickles all caught at the apogee of swing, myriads of sun-glinted moons, a motif not merely decorative but essential; the immobile or undecodable masks, all purposed universally, answered him—all suspended parts, hung from some ghostly rack of purpose, the clank, clatter, the assembly line of hunger, these answered Targ. "They don't know. I do." It was all meaningless, he thought back. He turned downhill and walked.

Mr. Kairos followed. Targ wished Mr. Kairos could let him alone, but he came after, whistling now in a low, meaningless, and unstructured expiration of sound that was hoarse-sounding because there was a bubble or a gurgle in the back of his throat. The noise made everything seem sad. Targ began to walk faster to get away from it. Mr. Kairos managed to follow, it being downhill, and keep whistling. The road ended in the beach sand.

Targ turned to the right, thinking it must only be a few miles around the swell-height of the island to the town. He began to walk beside the sea as fast as he could. Targ had the advantage; he was years younger and wore sneakers. After a while the whistling stopped and was replaced by panting, but still Mr. Kairos managed to keep up. They hit a stretch where something had gouged out a great trench; it was a rocky groove, a miniature ravine. The sand had been cleared off the sides, which descended about twenty feet. There was deep sand on the floor. The walls were made up of enormous stones, each weighing tons. They were intricately edged and joined together in perfect fits; how had they done that by hand alone? Targ couldn't see the sea from here but could hear, very clearly, the beat of the breakers on the beach. The heat was intense. The air wavered and flowed and lensed reality. **It seemed as if he was looking down a vast tunnel, westward, to and over a valley which sunk down thousands and thousands of feet. On the other side of the deep was a hazed-over cliff, on top of which sat a Gibraltar-shaped rock, and flowing past was a vast waterfall pouring down into a valley. Now, once the whole basin of the Mediterranean had been dry and then, one day, the Atlantic had broken in, through, and started to pour down, and in thousands of years had filled the basin.** He turned and said, "Look at that." But Kairos didn't seem to notice.

From here they couldn't see the green hill, but looking back along the cut, they could see the little temple on top—which was peculiar since the ravine was at an angle to the temple. It was almost as if in some way these stones were even the foundation of the temple. From this distance the temple looked white again. There were shells and fossils of all sorts embedded in the stone sides of the trough, arranged in patterns which made no sense. Targ wondered how they had got shells into the stone. The sand was softer at the bottom center of the trough and Targ walked through it deliberately, leading Mr. Kairos along. Mr. Kairos was wheezing now, following after, taking deep, rattling breaths now and then, but Targ wouldn't slow down. Targ thought he heard Mr. Kairos ask, "Why don't we get out of this?" Targ knew there was a sea breeze over his head, blocked by the sides, but he went on. The heat in the trough was furious, reflected by the shiny rock surfaces and countless particles of sand, broiling everything, focusing light, refocusing it, shooting it back and forth from side to side, concentrating on them. Soon Targ was dripping and dirty, but the gritty feel of sweat and sand felt good. His sneakers were full of sand. His feet were being abraded.

They must have gone on like this for a mile and soon Targ didn't hear anything behind him. He stopped and turned around. Mr. Kairos had fallen behind. He came on slowly, doggedly, a few hundred feet back, helping himself with his cane, which kept sinking deeply into the sand, causing him to double over. While Targ waited, **a sudden, furious babble of sounds broke out: he heard voices, sighs, little screams, motors running, the slapping sound that wind makes on slack sails, hot and busy laughter, interminable but unclear discussions counterpointing it all, shrieks of children and of copulations, orders being barked, all thrown at Targ. He thought he was going mad and went quickly back to Mr. Kairos.** The sound stopped suddenly after he had gone a few steps, as though he had stepped out of a room. Mr. Kairos kept coming. His white suit was completely wet and particles of grain stained it in spots. His mustache was wet, hanging, and drops fell slowly off the ends and onto the sand, leaving brown spots. Sweat ran down from under his hat and teared along the lines of his face. Even his cane was slick with the sweat running down the handle to the ferrule. Grains of sand adhered in patches to the wood. Targ wondered what made him so tough.

"Well, I'm just a good walker." Mr. Kairos panted and smiled through the drops of sweat. "I always have been. It's good for one. One should exercise. I used to walk to . . . work and read while . . . I walked: four . . . miles a day."

And now, Targ thought, Mr. Kairos mocked *him;* why did he pretend he hadn't heard the sounds too? The concentration of heat and blank sky was parenthesized by the green grain on top of the ravine, making the air look bright blue, cobalt almost, shading into black, expecially around the edge of the sun and against the edges of the rim. Mr. Kairos's voice wavered but didn't break: it was only unclear, its intentions destroyed by the light, ambiguous in spite of the clarifying blaze. Targ tasted something thick—green and salty—and smelled the hot sand, which stunk like cloth scorched by a hot pressing iron. The light scatter of sand-dusted shells lay along the sandbanks, thrown in a haphazard rain, and Targ wondered if the sea ever rose high enough to fill the trough. Mr. Kairos was talking to him, but the roaring of blood in his ears, the exhaustion, prevented Targ from hearing sounds and words: only the sense of Mr. Kairos's smug note of accomplishment bothered him. Targ turned away and kept plodding. Soon they came to the end of the trough. The sand of the beach, being moister here, was firm and they now made good time. Mr. Kairos kept wheezing behind Targ, still pointing out what might interest Targ. Targ was beyond involvement, having already seen the only point of interest on the whole island, and that a cheap imitation, corroded on its hill; a sham that distance improved. Targ thought about the voices till he decided it could only have been the sound of blood in his ears. Far away, on the sea rim, a freighter went slowly by, its rusted sides bright orange and its smoke climbing almost straight up over the canted smokestack.

When they got back, they went to their rooms. It was almost

sunset. The shore of the mainland was already dark but, seen through Targ's window, the port lights were shining across the water. It looked appealing, full of a life Targ had never known, full of people, all sparkling too. Targ wondered if a carnival was going on there. What was the port celebrating? Targ had almost forgotten how sterile all those new buildings really were. And, Targ thought a little regretfully, there was no way of getting back till tomorrow.

Targ washed. He couldn't do a good job of it because of the basin. He kept spilling water on the floor and parts of him remained dirty, still sticky and unwashed, but he changed his clothes and went out. He was terribly hungry now. Before going down, he felt compelled to stop in front of Mr. Kairos's door, which was open. Targ knocked on the lintel. Mr. Kairos called to Targ to come in. He was laying in his bed; brilliantly striped pajama tops showed over the sheet which served as a blanket. It was too warm to need any more. "I'm going to eat and drink," Targ told him. "Perhaps a little dancing to a Viennese orchestra. A gay flirtation or two. A duel. A ride through paradise gardens. Whispered endearments for a lady's ear."

Mr. Kairos looked at Targ. Long and lean candy stripes accentuated his thinness unbearably. He lay with his head propped sadly on one hand. "I'm tired," Mr. Kairos told Targ. "It was a long walk today. I'm not as young as I used to be."

"That's why we should drink. It staves off."

"But still, too much . . . That hastens . . . I know, I've bent many an . . ."

The advice annoyed Targ. "And that's a good of another sort," Targ said. "But not really. Nothing as simple as that. Besides, I beat four jokers in a drinking contest last night. So much for the decadence of civilized man. They will be tired and very thirsty after today's hoeing . . ."

"Harvesting."

". . . and wanting revenge. In all fairness, could I withhold satisfaction? Think what they're thinking: the effete, civilized man beats them at their own game. . . ."

"Their satisfaction won't have a good effect on you. Especially . . ."

But Targ couldn't let Mr. Kairos go into it at great length. "Better to give," Targ said. "Or is there anything else to do you haven't told me about?"

Mr. Kairos sighed again. "In a few days more the harvest will be done. They will have the festival. The festival is fascinating, going back thousands of years. Of course, on the surface it appears to be Christian. . . ."

"Yes, yes, it is a lovely pagan remnant." Targ knew the text. The riotous urges of the blood and flesh dignified by the title "ritual" and passed down through the ages and enshrined finally in the anthology of anthropological golden legends. An expenditure of surplus energies; ledger at zero; no more. "I won't be here. I couldn't bear one extra day, even giving satisfaction."

"Oh," Mr. Kairos said and Targ could see it made him sad.

"Are you going to stay on?" Targ asked. He was impatient, but Mr. Kairos looked so miserable. The pathetic expression kept annoying Targ. Targ hoped Mr. Kairos wouldn't come back to the mainland with him. Didn't he know, Targ wondered, better than to wear pajamas like that? It almost seemed, in the candle twilight, as if the colors were dissolving into a pool with oily rainbow striations on old and stagnant waters.

"Well," Mr. Kairos said, and stopped for a second. "I'd like to stay. But . . ."

But, thought Targ, he'd like me to stay on with him and walk along while he gives those amateurish (Targ may have forgotten content, but he remembered, at least, that he was supposed to be an expert in these things) little talks about the ancient choreography of reapers, or speeches about the ancient—therefore mystic—qualities of that broken-down piece of fradulent marble, that cheap imitation (probably eighteenth century at that) on the hill, or walk around the endless green hill, or down along the hot beach, or sit in town and swelter while drinking, watching the rustics sit, bored, exhausted, glowering at evening. Was their festival really so wild? Targ doubted it. Nothing as wild as at the university.

"Are you staying in bed tonight?" Targ asked again, just to be polite.

"I think I'll rest tonight; I'm very tired."

Targ went out, shutting the door behind him. He heard the sound of something being said behind the door, or was it the sound false teeth made, or was it the latch clicking into place? Or was it simply because Targ expected Mr. Kairos to say something?

He remembered something. Mr. Kairos had got him into the temple but he had not managed to get Mr. Kairos in.

5

Did she come again and again? Targ couldn't remember. Home-brew was stronger than one ever realized . . . and more comforting than cocktails. Stupefied, in those days, Targ drifted in some slough of gray haze which robbed his bone and muscle of the volition to act. He used to be thankful there was no need to be thinkful. Drink-weakened or sex-drained, he drifted into some Sargasso of laziness where he would wake and fall asleep again, but remembered only that he must wake in time for the ferry, in time to leave the island forever. But it was a vague urgency. Once upon a time he woke—or suddenly he sat up, which woke him—and before his eyes could focus, he seemed to drown forever in that long-ago and crepuscular light beyond which a window faintly loomed and beyond the frame a scrim-thick grayness behind which was the mildly sparkling sea dulling, and beyond that nothing itself but grayness again. Once, long ago, it seemed that the grayness became like muslin curtains decaying, tattered by some sound, perhaps the whistle, or thousands of whistles, of the ferry which used to be echoed back by the flap of wings, the rustle of things wakened into a temporary and wistful febrility. Targ didn't know what it was then; he only hoped he wouldn't miss the ferry when the time of departure came and was almost inclined not to care. Had Kairos cast a spell over him?

Once in a while, he remembered, Mr. Kairos used to slide in to report—as excitedly as one could, caught in this soft jelly—about a newly found relic, a missing marble hand, a mortuary crypt, a sarcophagus placed only a little way down in the sea where it wouldn't get in the way of the peasants. Or did Targ think it was the drinkers, like stiff monoliths, sitting, brooding, hands on knees, staring with ageless patience across the rivers of drink; had Mr. Kairos discovered only these? He tried to avoid Mr. Kairos by playing the lotus eater in those days, until he would really be sleeping, dreaming, lulled by the hypnotic voice of Mr. Kairos's urgent communiqués. Echoes of years he never paid attention to drifted in and pressed upon him: newspaper tags, things read, admonitions to be up and doing, a long page of an account book that showed him that finally the time would come—no matter how slowly it evolved—when they would be eroded of many ancient curses, geases, compulsions, or the tyranny of bio-logical forms; and yet all these, the comfort of knowing things to be done even if not done, lulled. Why struggle? Once there seemed to be an endless discussion, and that lasted many years, of nagging realities: the safe world-view of the Egyptians and the measured compass of the Greeks and the perverse joy of the Etruscans; and he used to struggle to unmire himself, to come to life, but this history drugged him. He would comfort himself, thinking that, after all, it was not too much time that passed, but only the few lanugo-distorted minutes he floated on, he, spread out and, like a sopped-up blot, absorbed into ages which had dissolved into the soft and suppurating grayness, the division between any now and any then, any him and any other gone. He remembered discovering his watch, an act as difficult as heaving oneself slowly up to peer at an enormous gnomon of a sundial made for giants, which didn't work then because the sun was unwound, and then, after months of struggle, he would look at it and then he would settle down and become immediately sure he had not looked and he would try to patience himself to wait for a little sunlight and then, once or twice, he looked at it, but it forever (at first it misled him because he didn't remember it entroping . . . but if it had entroped, how could he remember?) pointed at four thirty-two.

Mr. Kairos, Targ noticed, kept coming in like a metal man who strikes the hours and sat by Targ's side, looked at him anxiously and talked. But Targ couldn't be sure. Mr. Kairos's face kept coming closer and then receding in the haze. And Targ thought that, in other seasons, the three-eyed girl used to come and visit him. Her or Helen. It came to the same thing. They were sent. They fought over him. He thought she would lie beside him, looking at him, always looking at him. What if they stole his money while he was in this state? he wondered. But it didn't make him very anxious.

Once upon a time Mr. Kairos came in and, almost dying, Targ thought, decided to pour out some long, endlessly complicated story about how he had lost job and history and found . . . was it God, or a loved one? or had he been found? He used to stop frequently to look at Targ, as if waiting for an answer. But Targ had forgotten it all. Targ remembered blurring something at him, something conventional, trying to make it, if nothing else, comforting. But Targ could never understand what Mr. Kairos was getting at, only that he was in some sort of terrible distress, probably physical, like ulcers, or cancer, and quite like a child who wanted him to do something. Senile? And he would resent Kairos for breaking down in this punctual way when he should be strong. Then, always remembering with an effort, Targ would sit up and demand to know of the empty, dusty room how many days had passed, really, and had they missed the ferry, and if so, how many times? He interrupted Mr. Kairos and questioned him carefully—even though the words didn't come out clearly: had the ferry stopped running many years ago? Mr. Kairos lost the drift of what he was trying to say—after many a day Targ would remember those times and daydream about them—while he assured Targ that the ferry was still running. And then—Targ couldn't be sure in what year that happened—he used to fall asleep again.

6

When Targ woke, the sun was high. They were gone. Targ looked out across the water but could not see the mainland, he thought, because of the stickiness in his eyes. A gummy mote floated there for a moment on his eyeball. There was something about the sky itself that seemed, though still blue, faintly hazed over. Targ rubbed his eyes and shook his head. The dimness persisted even though his eyes were clear; as though muslin had been dropped over—no, *in*—his eyes. Targ looked at his watch. It wasn't running. He was sure it was late morning. For a second he wasn't sure if it was the day the ferry would be leaving, or the day the ferry was to come. He realized he had slept for at least a day and then he began to worry about missing some appointment. What? Yes. Helen. What else? He would have to hurry or miss the ferry. Targ wondered if Mr. Kairos was leaving too. Or was he simply not calling Targ, hoping Targ would miss the ferry and stay on with him? Targ was annoyed. He dressed quickly, packed his few items into his small bag. Targ went into the hallway. Kairos's door was open. Targ looked in.

Mr. Kairos lay on his bed. He was not, Targ could see quite clearly now, definitely not Professor Biddle. How could he have ever thought such a thing? The bed, which had neither headboard nor footboard, had been pushed to the middle of the room. Against one of the walls was an elaborately carved chest of drawers. Graceful angels, entwined in congress with crippled devils, were bas-reliefed on the panels. Elaborate flower and grass work ran around the edges; acanthus leaves, flames connected into framework with endless ivy garlands. And within that a continuous and infinite rose and prickle motif, circled eternally. The ornamentation was cracked off here and there, showing raw wood, but all had been polished year after year, age after age, into a roseate brown that glistened faintly and showed a multiplicity of lights scattered, subtly, all over the surface facing the door. On top of the chest was a rude clay basin surrounded by old-fashioned shaving tools: straight razor and long brush. There was a pack of American chewing gum, opened and three-fifths empty. Beside the gum was a glass in which teeth floated hilariously. Targ looked again and wondered how he could ever have mistaken Mr. Kairos for Professor Biddle.

A pinch-top satchel was in a clear space on the floor. A few cloth items—towels, washcloths, seersucker pants—hung out and flowed limply down the light-brown leather sides to the floor. The bed itself was neatly made, without covers or pillow, draped only with a sheet which hung stiffly to the floor. In the morning-hazy room the bed looked like a white slab. Mr. Kairos's white suit was hung on a hanger, and that hung to the window frame, blocking the light and casting a long shadow on the floor. Mr. Kairos wore only the bottoms of his pajamas; the top was sprawled, buttons down, on the floor on the side of the bed opposite to where the satchel lay.

Whatever Professor Biddle (he meant Mr. Kairos) had taken had contorted his body terribly and erased any possible resemblance to Professor Biddle. His thick lock of hair drooped down and split the forehead, fell further over the bridge of his nose and made his gaze seem cross-eyed. Mr. Kairos's left leg was flung out to the side over the edge of the bed. But the knee muscles had tightened and held the leg rigidly in place, the foot a few inches above the floor. His body was turned to his right so that he looked as if he had been trying to rise. His left arm crossed his body as though he had thrown it there to assist his rise; his right hand was thrust out stiffly, balancing the jut of the left leg. The right fist, fingers upward, was half clenched. There was a little apothecary's bottle in the hand. It had been crushed by the strength of the final agony. Had the body overruled the mind's decision after the pill had been swallowed, and tried to live? Between the clawed fingers—each cramped muscle in the wrist still showed, tightly spasming those fingers—Targ could see glistening splinters of glass, the powdery green of the pills, and the blood congealed, crusted into hook shapes around where the glass had entered the flesh of the palm.

There was no fat on the trunk. The bones of the rib cage started through the dead-white skin, and where the body bent, the flesh lay in fatless little skin rolls. The face looked upward, surprisingly calm, negating the violent disturbance of the body. The eyes were piously rolled upward, inward, half submerged under the upper lids, looking above and toward the wall behind the head's crown, seeing something there, something the eyes had had to look at very badly before death. Targ looked there. There was nothing on that wall now but the light of the hazy sun raying around the bent-forward shoulders of the hanging suit, making—because of the color and the angle to the floor—a green gnomon that flickered, caused to dance and waver by the heat of the sun on the air. There was a strong stink of shit. From the opening in his pajama pants, the erect and shockingly young penis stuck out. Targ looked up to see if Kairos had sprayed the ceiling.

Targ hadn't thought Kairos had it in him to do such a thing. Trag heard a giggle. Trag wouldn't accept the brutality of that giggle. "Well, old fart . . ." and the shocking giggle came again. "Well, old fart, what an exhibition of yourself," Targ said. Giggled: killed himself: stupid old fart.

But he couldn't help thinking that if Targ didn't leave right away he would miss the ferry and be stuck on the island after all. He thought of what Targ would have to go through: the wait, the police interrogation, the endless time spent waiting, the possibly . . . no, the *certainly* missed ferry, another two days waiting, to say nothing of the time riding across the gulf to the port; and Helen there, or Helen gone, or Helen missed, or Helen come here; the explanations. . . . Targ looked out the window over the puffed-out suit shoulder. He couldn't see the port from this room, only the expanse of island, green hill, still grain-covered, the butterflies gaily staining everything, a few cypress trees near the top around the little temple. But what if he left? What would they think? Well, it was so obviously suicide. And as for the rest of it—motive, their opinions—none of it mattered.

The dead stare made Targ look again at the crumpled suit. The white linen was creased and grain-stained, bent, holding shape. The sleeves flexed slightly and the pants legs bent back a little at the knees. Two flies buzzed around the room. One landed on Targ's face and flew away as his face muscle twitched. It landed on Kairos's face and crawled, in short, aimless rushes, till it was on the smooth of the forehead. The eyes seemed to cross as if trying to focus on the fly. A sleeve of the suit was fluttered upward by an intermittent breeze that slipped through the window. . . . The other fly landed on the tip of the penis. Targ blinked. Trag heard the giggle. Targ waved his hands and the flies flew away. Targ started to leave. Let them find him; Kairos's dead; it's pointless; let them find him and bury him; it doesn't matter; it really doesn't matter, Targ thought.

Targ went downstairs. They had paid for a week so he didn't have to settle with the owner. The streets were empty now; even the children were gone. Targ walked slowly down to the wharf, walking with a stately step. His head was half turned as if he expected to hear a sudden call from behind. The ferry was still there. Gulls fought over something in the adjacent sands. Clouds of flies hovered over pieces of rotting seaweed close to the water's edge. Targ marched down the long wharf, past the warehouse. A sailor was sitting on one of the pierheads; he nodded at Targ as solemnly as his thick neck would permit. Along the edge of the wharf lay pieces of shell, almost empty of flesh, covered with little fly hordes. The ferry rocked slowly in the water. The sky was still blue, but tinged with white, and the air had become totally still. Targ could hear the muted breakers and, beyond the boat, he could see waves forming far out and moving in dignified long marches to break against the island. Flies danced across the air and landed on him. He brushed them off. The slow wave lines advanced, bearing up and sinking down wrack—weed, kelp, bladders, jellyfish, pieces of wood—moving it all majestically landward to be thrown up on the beaches to dry on the sand, rot, and be consumed.

Trag put down his bag and turned back. He told the sailor, as he repassed, that he would return in a little while. The sailor told Targ that there was no hurry, there were a few hours left before the boat departed. For a second that urgent sense, that panic, that feeling that he should be somewhere else, that there was something he had not done, possessed Targ. He should not turn back. He looked at the fly wings shimmering in the hazy sunlight and forced himself to be calm.

7

The officer sat behind his desk. He was wearing his frayed uniform. The desktop was empty except for a blank daily report form; next to it lay a crumpled, dirty handkerchief. The plaster walls had yellowed notices on them; a few photographs, faded into sepia, of uniformed officials. Behind the officer, a door led to another room. There was a black line on the floor running across the room about four feet in front of the black, chipped desk. Targ went up to the desk. The officer's hat was off; his thick, light hair, soft and waveless, limp, fell lankly across his forehead. He looked young. He would be bald early. The officer looked up and smiled, happy to see Targ; certainly eager to talk. But he restrained himself, in keeping with the sense of his importance, in the name of duty. "It is hard to fill out a day's report when nothing happens."

"Something's happened," Targ told him.

The officer shrugged. "Of course. Someone has stolen something. You Americans go everywhere. You carry the wealth of the world with you. You tempt. You lay traps. Then our people, who have never thought of deviating from uprightness, are taught . . . imagination. They steal."

"You said they stole something once."

"Once." The officer said it contemptuously. "Once. What is once? How serious was it? Amber. An aberration," he said and shrugged his shoulders again. He sighed and reached down, pulled open a drawer, pulled out a small printed slip of paper, waved it to shake off the dust. "You see how this testifies to the high incidence of crime on this island?" He put it on his desk and sighed. "What was stolen?"

"My friend has killed himself."

"Please stand behind the black line," the officer told Targ. He said it so fast that it seemed to be spoken almost simultaneously with Targ's words.

Targ looked at him, not understanding.

"The black line," the officer said, leaning over his desk and pointing downward. "There."

Targ looked at his feet and to either side, but saw nothing.

"No. There! The black line. There! There! *There!* Therethere-there!" the officer shouted and his finger stabbed again and again at a place behind Targ.

Targ turned and saw it and turned back again and smiled at the officer. The officer was excited, serious.

"Please, behind the line."

Targ moved back a few steps.

"Now," the officer said. He breathed deeply to calm himself and stood up. "Wait a moment."

And of course this was predictable, even traditional. "Please hurry. I have to leave today."

The officer looked at Targ carefully; his eyelids narrowed joyfully.

"It's not as callous as it sounds. He was not really my friend. We met accidentally, traveling. We decided to visit this place together. That's all," Targ explained.

"But wait," the officer said. He turned and went through the door behind the desk. Targ lit a cigarette and looked around. The room held a filing cabinet; the desk was planted between the wall and the window (which looked out at the church wall a foot away). Everything except the desk was painted white. The officer came back after a while. He had changed his clothes. He now wore a splendid blue uniform with red piping and with a tight high collar which pinched his neck a little. He wore a new cap set tightly and squarely down on his head. His hair was neatly brushed in place now. A revolver holster and a wooden truncheon were suspended from his shining belt. He sat down. "Now then, you will repeat what you have told me," he said. He picked up the crumpled handkerchief and put it into a bottom drawer.

"There's nothing to tell. I was going to leave—"

The officer looked at his watch. "It is twelve twenty-three. Please go on," he said and made a note in his day's report, pushed it to one side, opened another drawer in his desk, reached in, rummaged around, and pulled out some forms, rattled them, shaking dust loose from the bunch. He laid them out, one set of forms on top of the other, but with each edge showing, like a pack of cards riffled loosely.

Targ remembered his suitcase and worried about it; it was worthless, but he worried.

"As you see, I am the sole representative of authority here. I am police and customs and government; the mayor, the bureau of the census and"—he grinned quickly, like a light snapping on and off—"the manifestation of my country's power, civilization: the army, to say nothing of the navy. Thus I must record for each department's interest the particular and applicable happening." The quick grin made him look, for that second, like a little boy; and then he was serious again, stiffer, older. "A bore. Necessary. Please go on. Most of my country's power abroad was lost because there was no attention paid to such details. Please go on."

"I was going back to the mainland—"

"What time was this?"

"I don't know. Half an hour ago. I was leaving for the ferry—"

"Don't you have a watch?"

"It stopped."

"Who ever heard of such a thing? An American without the time?"

"I forgot to wind it. I do that frequently," Targ told him. "The point of my vacation was to forget about time." He got the feeling that the sailor was opening his suitcase and going through it, handling each item, and he had to hurry. It didn't really matter. He had nothing of value there. He had to remind himself.

The officer was enjoying the exasperating role he was playing. "Then what time do you think it was when you got through killing your friend?" he asked suddenly.

"He wasn't my friend," Targ said and sighed. He was going to miss the ferry. The officer was going to play games: he had to. The officer was going to hope it was murder, hang on to that hope, and then, after taking an endless time about it, resign himself to the fact that Kairos had indeed committed suicide.

"Why are you blinking?"

"Foul play was suspected," Targ said.

"I beg your pardon?"

"Shouldn't you get a priest, an undertaker, something?"

"You haven't answered my question."

Targ decided not to answer the question. He waited.

"What good will a priest do? You say he's a suicide. Is he a Catholic?"

"I don't know."

"You see," the officer said and smiled. "Now—"

"Look, at this rate I'm going to miss the ferry."

"Why are you in such a rush?" the officer asked softly. Targ saw the sly little smile, that almost derivative, literary, but nevertheless efficacious smile of cunning. A boat whistle sounded; had Targ missed the ferry after all? But what had he expected? Had he really expected to come in and say, "He has committed suicide," and then, after at most one or two questions, be permitted to go off to the mainland? Had he been so simple? A peculiar reversion to an innocence lost when he had changed himself. He knew better. He had been all over Europe. He knew about bureaucracies. He could do no better now than to resign himself. Tradition demanded it. But that he understood that the ferry was irrevocably missed, and that he must be here now for two . . . no, three days (counting today), did not diminish but increased his impatience. And Targ knew that the officer would see those signs: the fidgeting, the annoyance, the quick glances at his watch, which didn't work, the nervous hand exploring his pocket (possibly for a bribe), certainly because of a suspiciously intolerable itch, and the officer would (it must be expected, at least for a while) interpret those manifestations as signs of guilt. Targ couldn't help himself.

So Targ told the officer what little he knew about Kairos; after all, they had just met. And answering, or trying to, such questions about Kairos as "What sort of a man was he?" didn't restore the dead man to Targ, but did make him remember and tell the officer about the initial meeting, the confusion with Professor Biddle, his old inductor, and he paused to wonder how he could have made such a mistake, and wondered why he was going into it at all. . . . Yes, that would explain why they, strangers, had come to be traveling together. Though Targ did take great care not to tell the officer that he was going to leave without reporting the death: he knew what that would lead to.

"But who was this man?" the officer asked again and again. How little Targ knew. Kairos was a retired, silly, pompous old man, a businessman with a penchant for ancient airs and dances. The officer looked perplexed at that and asked again, "But who was this man?" as if it were only a matter of stimulating a recalcitrant memory, as if Targ really knew and wouldn't tell. Targ could see Kairos on the bed again and worried about the flies, kept blinking, had to be asked, each time more suspiciously, that same question again and again. How should he expect Targ to know who this man was? And then Targ had to answer a lot of questions about himself. This time he took great care not to explain the reasons for his trip, his . . . ah . . . disturbance. Disturbance could be equated with personal psychological breakdown; breakdown could lead to murder. When the officer had finished writing, it seemed as if the whole thing had taken hours. "Can I go now?" Targ asked, worrying about the suitcase and wondering if they had taken it. And if they had, would they give it to Helen if she happened to meet the boat at the pier?

"No. We have to view the body."

"But where can I—"

"The body must be identified. . . . You don't understand your position," the officer said. "We still don't know that you haven't murdered him." And Targ could see that joyousness and excitement made the officer's face look boyish, intense, almost poetic again, every time he considered this delicious proposition. It was, after all, this kind of enthusiasm Targ had to fear. The young face pleaded for complicated and murderous possibilities. What joy the officer would take in the apprehension of the cunning murderer; how it would all break the deadly spell of this sleepy place; how gratefully he could embellish his forms with details . . . practically write a novel.

So they went out and down the silent street to the little pension. Targ was not yet prisoner and murderer, but not quite a free man. His status wavered between that of an innocent man who was a citizen of a great power—and that would not work to his advantage—and a criminal to whom the officer must be both grateful and brutal. It was odd walking through those empty streets. When they got to the pension they saw two natives standing across the street, their arms folded, watching.

"Yes, they're here," said the officer. "I don't know how they *know*. It's a serious sign, my friend, if they spare two from the harvest to observe."

They went into the pension and up the stairs to Kairos's room. Targ had forgotten to close the door; they walked in. It . . . he . . . was still there. There were more flies in the room now. Targ started to brush away the flies but the officer stopped him. "Don't touch him," he said in a melodramatic voice. His lips were compressed. He played it for all it was worth, his face arranged into that all-seeing, noncommittal immobility policemen all over the world wore. A convention, Targ thought, which subtracts from the police face its peculiar individuality.

The officer walked around the corpse carefully, examining everything he could, but it was all too obvious and a little disappointing. One turn around the body was enough to make everything clear. The three or four additional circlings were gratuitous, Targ thought, done for the discipline and theater of it. How many times had Targ read about it, seen them do it this way in movies, in plays, on television? And yet the profundity of deductive reasoning, the traditions and rituals of detection, the whole sacred body of detective literature couldn't mystify this situation, couldn't turn up the hint, the something subliminal that implied . . . *all.* Nothing could turn the disappointing moment into anything more sinister. Unless desire for results and redressing of imbalances bred perversity and injustice; that too was common. It was all tawdry, comical, surprising to see that people did what they were supposed to do, what was expected of them. Except, of course, for himself, Targ, and Kairos. The officer's sense of impotence made him look solemnly at that ridiculous, that wistful thing, Targ thought. The inability to see the humor of it caused the officer to look again, as if the looking, in the absence of a "crime," would make it all poetic and the poetry would transform the causes of the deed. The officer knelt, rose, moved in a half squat crabwise, knelt. At one point he appeared to be sighting over the stiff penis.

The officer turned to the hanging suit and went through the pockets. He rifled the suitcase. He examined the identification material, nodded his head judiciously, as though he had uncovered new mysteries, and put it all into his pocket. The old man had a lot of money; the officer put that into his pocket too. "He is a Catholic," he told Targ as an afterthought. He said, "I will confiscate the money till we may determine how to dispose of it. There seem to be no relatives, at least none are indicated in any of the papers. He was quite alone, had no one, except for you."

Me?

"Get a priest, then."

"Is that what he'd have liked?"

"How would I know? He wasn't mine."

"But at any rate he's a suicide," the officer said and sighed, admitting it. "I suppose you may go," he told Targ. Targ waved his hand over the body to brush away the flies. "Don't touch him," the officer said.

"Then get an undertaker."

"There is no such thing on this island. Nothing like this has ever happened."

"Who takes care of the dead?"

"The natives. They suffer the priest to say the proper words, but—"

"Get one of them."

"They won't do it. They only bury their own."

"Well, it's none of my business. At least cover him," Targ snapped and left. When he got into the street the worry that they had taken the suitcase bothered him again. He began to walk fast, almost to trot. Targ met the priest and when he asked about Mr. Kairos, told him to go to the pension. Targ kept walking very fast. He knew the ferry had gone. It was pointless to hurry. He couldn't help responding to the sense of impatience, of panic that kept working inside him.

Of course the ferry was gone. It had gone at least an hour ago. And perhaps, yes, probably that was why the officer had permitted him to leave so easily. Targ could still see it in the water, far away, flanked by mocking pleasure boats, overshadowed by the huge warships, steaming away but not seeming to move at all, caught partway between the island and the mainland. Targ watched it for a long time till it grew quite small, small enough to be mistaken for one of the pleasure boats. Targ thought that if he had a motorboat, he might catch the ferry yet . . . might even go to the mainland itself.

Beyond the ferry the air had gotten mistier and Targ couldn't see the mainland. The sailor had left his suitcase on the pier after all. There was a gull sitting on it. It flew away with a sudden squawk when Targ came near. Its launching knocked over the suitcase as it lumbered heavily, flapping its great, clumsy wings, almost as though it were trying to walk through the air rather than fly. It gained speed and began to rise beyond the edge of the pier, turned, became light and graceful, emitting triumphant or derisive mewls from its hooked beak. Targ shook his fist at the soaring bird and picked up his suitcase. He went back along the pier, back alongside the long warehouse, up the street and back to the pension. Even though it was too late to leave, the sense of urgency and expectancy would not stop.

8

Targ walked. There was nothing to do now. He was trapped on the island. He wondered if Helen would come running to see what had happened to him, or would she extend permissiveness just a little longer and bide? Whatever she did, it would be the wise thing, the right thing, the infuriating thing. Targ, angry, would not be loved. He could only wait it out. He passed the pension, walked in, left the suitcase in the hallway, and went outside again.

Targ walked through the town and out and up the narrow road. It was long past midday now. The light turned yellower, thicker, and in turn cast yellowness over everything. The harvesters had almost got to the middle road and would, in a little while, pass across it and start down the other side of the island, harvesting into the east. Their faces looked worried now. The smooth rhythm of their scything movements was broken by a sense of still-mild frenzy. Even children had joined them. They watched for their rain spirit. Were their swing-end stares for *him* now, instead of being thrown over their shoulders? Those stares lingered just a second-fraction longer, slowing them just a little. The women worked with their skirts tucked into their belts. The brown, sweat-gleaming thighs were grain-speckled and dirt-smudged. The women cut as strongly as the men, but all of them seemed not to get through with it any faster: those smooth and enviable rhythms were now made erratic by panic, the mathematical precision of their line's movement broken. Targ looked for the three-eyed woman, Cyclops' daughter, among them. She was not there. Of course; she would defile and infect the crop.

Targ turned and looked down the hill behind him. Far down, the fishing boats' painted stares peered at the reapers, the sea, the sky, him.

Targ climbed to the top of the hill and sat on a crumbling temple step. He could see the whole bent sweep of the reapers' line move ahead less inexorably, the light flashing faintly from the sickles, duller now, ragged, in no longer perfect and unified timed intervals; the sounds of slicing hisses reached Targ's ears like clock ticks. Targ looked around the horizon's edge. He couldn't see the port or the mainland. It was gone, completely lost in a horizon that fused into a blank orange wall: the seamainlandportsky, all one. Boats running a little closer to the island were suspended in the haze, gaining and losing reality as they manifested themselves out of the overcast, passing, yellowing out into nothingness. Three fleets of landing boats at three points around the island edged forward, went backward, jockeyed for position, came in and out of the nothingness. Flights took off from or landed on the aircraft carriers. There was a constant hum of aircraft. He looked at the mistiness and thought that at last they had woven a complete canopy of contrails overhead. He shook his fist at the fleets and wondered if binoculars or telescopes were trained on him.

Sounds played tricks, seeming to come from a long distance or, surprisingly, from quite close, sometimes from the temple itself. What they almost said had nothing to do with the fact that they were far or close. They came with greater frequency now and Targ wondered if they had anything to do with the weather. Or, tired now, too weary to panic, he wondered if his disturbance was entering a new phase. He crumbled his cigarette and the coal fell to the step, where it glowed before burning out, leaving a brown stain. He went to sleep for a while and dreamed that one of those ridiculous voices, a cross between a child's and a woman's, came out from the temple, singing some long, some interminable song about love and desertion, but Targ couldn't catch the words: he inferred them from the rhythm and pitch of the voice.

9

Targ woke in the evening, stiff and hungry. The reapers had left the fields. Perhaps tradition had driven them in. Tradition grew out of survival and overcame it; how well he knew that. That, or because of the danger of hurting one another with their sickles in the dark. The yellow haze had reddened toward the west. It was almost night around Targ. To the east, gay cherry, lemon, and lime boat lights bobbed. To the west, pale lights rose and fell in the heaving sea swells. In America, Targ thought, remembering what Kairos had said about progress, they would have mounted lights in the fields and kept on harvesting, illuminating dark hours with a fine impartiality. Targ tried to move, but for a while all he could do was lean against one of the pillars, look to the darkness, and suffer the pillar flutings to cut into his back. He waited for it to become completely dark. He was still groggy, too tired to move. Soon there was nothing left but the sound of wind rustling the grain, shuffling the cypress leaves, the constant and soft stridulation of the insects and the dull hum of aircraft. Off and on, the sudden and startling gabble of voices came, like a radio dial being flipped casually from station to station, across the band of possibility. After a while Targ forced himself to stand. He swayed and almost fell, teetered, lurched a few feet, and began to move. He walked down the road. The town crouched, squat and black, far beneath the hill, crusted with dim lights. As he walked the digestive juices were released and he realized that he hadn't eaten for a long time.

As Targ came into town, the men stood around in silent groups staring up at the sky. They didn't speak to one another, but the air seemed full of talk. A great babbling communion in which the same questions were asked again and again, each possibility debated endlessly. Targ wondered: did they know? Did they mourn Kairos? Was their way of looking at the sky a form of silent tribute? He doubted it. No longer did they have that aimless look of idleness and boredom, though to the casual glance their attitudes seemed unchanged. Targ wondered what disturbed them.

No doubt reminiscences were being exchanged: the older ones dug far back in their memories and remembered terrible events. Days of disaster. Years of hunger. What had Kairos said? Before the war, wind, rain, and rot had ruined the reaping. They had burned the church. Did they remember that? Did they discuss that? Did they silently threaten? As Targ passed, their silence intensified. Though they never turned their eyes from the sky, the unmanifest rain spirit, some minor but terribly alert aspect of their attention tracked Targ carefully, curiously, wondering what to make of him. Silence passed with him like the trough of a wave. And when he had gone, he was sure they broke out again in furious and voiceless conversation.

Possibly they commiserated with Targ's loss. He thought sardonically: Targ's loss. It was no great loss, Targ thought at them, explaining that it all didn't really matter. Women stood in the doorways, black shawls over their heads now, hooded creatures; their great dark eyes watching the men for cues, not looking at the sky; possibly forbidden to look at the rain spirit. They saw rain through their men's stares.

Targ passed the church. He looked in. It was almost empty. The inside was simple; it consisted of a square room containing two rows of benches arranged traditionally in parallel lines turned toward the altar. Along one wall the darkness of empty niches was crinkled by the flickering of the lamp. The altar itself was covered with a surprisingly clean rich maroon cloth trimmed with gold fringe. Behind the altar, bolted to the wall, was a huge wooden cross to which was tied a statue. Targ went a little closer, along the side of the church. No one was in the church but the priest, whom he mistook for one of the women because he had put a black shawl over his head and was praying to the statue on the cross. The thing was huge, incredibly huge, about twenty feet high, and was lashed to the cross with black ropes. Targ couldn't see the statue clearly, but it wasn't Christian, not the Jesus. Possibly it was ancient Greek, Roman, or even Sumerian, pitted, eroded, made indeterminate by wearing away. Its definition was given it more by what had been done to it, the context it was in, than what it really was. Probably this replaced the other Jesus, the one Kairos said had been burned. They couldn't burn this one, Targ thought. A beard of crude wavy lines was painted on the face. The blind, blank eyeballs had sockets which had once held semiprecious stones and were now painted with pupils, dots really . . . too small. It made the expression appear to glare in indignation rather than sorrow. The original arms and legs were missing. New legs and arms, much too short for the head and torso, had been added, with the conventional wounds painted on. These limbs were made out of wood but painted a pinkish white to simulate the marble tones of the trunk. The paint didn't match the marble. In reality the statue might have been, when originally carved, in any position at all. Perhaps it was even one of those statues whose disappearance had worried Mr. Kairos so much.

Targ waited for the priest to finish, but he kept praying. Bored, finally, Targ left and went back to the pension.

10

The suitcase was still in the hallway when Targ got back. He picked it up and went upstairs. He passed Kairos's door. The officer and the priest were in the room. How had the priest gotten there ahead of him? The body lay between them, still uncovered. Targ thought he smelled something heavy and sweet, this sweetness mingling with the fading smell of shit, hovering in the unmoving air of the room. The officer and the priest were carrying on a discussion whose sense Targ couldn't make out although he understood the words. By their gestures and expressions, a series of statements disagreeable to both, they made to each other. Angry tones. Sharp gestures. Targ had the impression they had begun to talk a fraction of a second after he entered but the slight weariness, the touch of routine in their motions indicated they had been arguing for a long time. Targ watched them. Caught in his peripheral vision, something off to the side moved. Someone was sitting in an alcove of shadows.

They disliked one another, but that didn't matter; the argument was ancient. From time to time one or the other would break off the discussion, stride to the window, and stare out, peering over the shoulders of Kairos's still hanging suit. Air-filled, an arm-sleeve shook; the stomach ballooned, collapsed; the pants legs were agitated. The suit danced back and forth. Almost too tired to move, Targ watched them talking. Watched them gesturing, but rarely looking at the body, failing to notice, in the fury of their argument, flies accreting. Targ got used to the second smell; he wasn't even sure if it was a smell rather than the expectation of a smell. He dropped the suitcase. They turned, startled at the sound, and seemed, by some sort of secret and unexpressed agreement, to rearrange the expression of their differences, as if determined not to argue so furiously in front of a stranger. Targ came over to Kairos, waved his hand over the body. The flies all flew away. He reached down, picked up the ends of the sheet, and drew it over the body. Had he driven away all the flies?

The priest looked almost like an islander. He was short, the way they all were, with great heaviness of bone; the thickness of his face muscles showed beneath the layer of skin glazed over with a patina of boredom that parched the flesh. But he wore round, gold-rimmed glasses. The lips were thin, pursed, as if compressed to contain a disapproval he must not show; they were a little too red, as if bitten or made up. He nodded to Targ, shrugged his shoulders, and said, "It is regrettable." He ducked his head. The nod, Targ supposed, stood for the whole possible range of sympathy. The priest's accent was not as purely mainland as the officer's; something alien and guttural had invaded it. Had he been there longer or was he a better mimic? "Do you have any idea why he did it?" he asked. "Was he depressed? Did he have some sort of spiritual crisis?"

Of course he would ask that, Targ thought, and tried to remember what crisis Kairos might have had. "Spiritual" was not a word that came easy to Targ: he was never sure what it really meant (unless discussing a book, of course, or characters in a book). He tried to remember that prim, this fussy old man, the almost bald man with his one thick youthful lock of hair. Pedantic tones counterpointed by mewls of the attendant sea gulls . . . and Targ's preoccupations being nibbled away at. Spiritual? Trag could have understood spiritual crises, but then Trag had been a passionate amateur. Targ looked at the shrouded body but he couldn't even remember clearly what Kairos had looked like a few hours ago. "I don't know. I didn't notice." Targ wanted to go over and lift up the cover and take a look again; perhaps he would remember, or perhaps he had overlooked a fly beneath the sheet. Spiritual? He stepped closer. The wind fluttered the sleeve of the suit; the suit writhed like a spastic, or a sail. The officer saw the movement out of the corner of his eye and went over to look out the window anxiously. "Maybe it will not come so soon. I can still see the stars."

"It is coming too fast. I believe it is all caused by those atomic explosions; those trails of smoke in the sky; man's temerity, usurping God's province . . . weather control . . . vast agricultural changes . . . jungles made into deserts: all these bring on weather like this. Man has taken over the devil's role: God-usurping America and Russia . . ." the priest said. "So now this . . . But you two were traveling together. How could you not know him?"

"We met on the mainland a few days ago quite casually. We decided to visit a few sites together on this island. That's all there is to it. I hardly knew him."

"Such a thing to do. And yet you must have had a closer bond? All men are responsible for one another. . . ."

"Are they?" Did he really believe that?

"I am told he was Catholic. Had he lapsed?"

Only into senility and comedy. "I told you, I don't know. Didn't he talk to you yesterday?"

"A word or two. I was busy with the consecration of the harvest. I was late getting to the beginning. Something had gone wrong with my clock . . . first time in fifteen years. They were close to beginning without the blessing." He leaned forward and turned his back to the shadows and whispered confidentially. Targ moved to see; the priest seemed to drift into his way accidentally. "It's what they have been looking for . . . a lapse. Serves them right." Targ tried to see who was sitting in the shadows. Great knobbed and gnarled hands clasped knees. Louder: "I couldn't pay attention. Perhaps I was even brusque. I was running through the service as quickly as I could—to catch up to them—and since their language is so difficult, I was having trouble. No mistakes are allowed, and I have never made mistakes (which would indicate the fallibility of the Church itself) . . . but the inflections, nuances, and tones are complicated and change with the small shifts of the seasons and great cycles, and . . . I should have seen he was in great distress. I might have done something for him. Who was to know? He said nothing; he showed nothing. He only questioned me about the ceremonies and, in fact, for a second I even thought he was trying to break them up."

"He had a lot of money with him," the officer said, coming back into the center of the room. The quick way he said it showed he hadn't given up the idea that Targ might have done it. Targ half turned his head to look at the officer. The priest continued to look at Targ. Targ stepped forward and looked into the shadows. It was an island peasant. He turned back. Yes, theft. That would resolve everything. After all, why in this day of credit would the dead man have carried so much money? Had the money been stolen?

"Did he? His relatives will be happy," Targ said, more to be polite than anything else, forgetting that Kairos had no relatives. "We paid our way separately." But still, Targ kept wondering what he would do for the rest of the night; and tomorrow; and the day after till the next ferry departed. And what if Helen came? If she did, would he have to show her the island? They would be bored together; they would bicker . . . and yet, he missed her. Perhaps he could get someone to sail them back to the mainland. A little sea voyage might be Honeymoon. He laughed. He shouldn't laugh. Once he had had a honeymoon, and believed in those things . . . but that wasn't with Helen. If not, they would be stuck; tedious, Targ thought, like long, endless Sunday afternoons. They would "do" the island quickly: see the temple, watch the reapers, go to the funeral. "I suppose there should be enough money to provide for a funeral?" Targ said to the priest.

"But there can't be a funeral. He can't be buried in consecrated ground." The priest's horror was ritual: the hands were thrown up (but not too high); an expression of distress on the face; the head shaken vigorously once, accentuated to impress upon Targ the impossibility of such an act.

"I forgot. You mean there can't be *your* kind of funeral. Somewhere else. It doesn't matter," Targ said. So it would be a civil ceremony; the mayor of the town—oh, yes, that was the officer—would say what must be said; eulogies to the unknown dead. It would not be impressive, but he and Helen (if she came) would watch that. Their hands folded at crotch level, their heads would bow perfunctorily; their eyes would look around from under their bent heads; their minds would keep quarreling furiously.

"He's in a state of sin. He's taken his life," the priest insisted on saying. "So there can't be any rites. . . ."

Targ nodded impatiently; he knew all the arguments. ". . . the great canon 'gainst self-slaughter . . ." A bore; Kairos had done the worst; Kairos had despaired; Kairos had taken God's dispensation out of God's hand; Kairos had romantically disposed of it himself; Kairos had pride . . . will. Trag would have called it pride. Trag was a romantic. Targ tried to remember what proud act Kairos had done. None; except if one counted that stubborn following through the sand . . . Targ sighed. The breeze blew in.

They all turned toward the wind-danced suit. Now the priest went over to look out. "It's hazy, I tell you, definitely hazy. What shall we do?" he asked and came back. He looked at the sheet and shook his head again, this time not so violently. But the head-shaking, although compassionate in style, was not for Kairos and perhaps indicated a little despair. Compassionate for whom? "Did he show any signs of repentance before he died?"

"Do you care?"

"Of course I care!"

"Do any of us care?"

"It's important to know."

Ecclesiastical voyeurism.

"I need a sign of repentance."

The *body* had shown repentance, but he knew the priest didn't believe in bodies. "I don't know. I was somewhere else. Still . . . another cemetery, then. Civil, Protestant, Jewish, pagan, a tower of silence. Anywhere. There must surely be a tower of silence here?"

"There is no other place on the island. You don't understand," the priest said. The muscles underneath the sheath of comfortable face flesh seethed; tough lumps beneath the pudgy, ameliorative surface.

"In the ocean then."

"That's terribly callous of you," the priest said, making himself look even more horrified and angry.

"It is not so much a matter of obsequies," the officer said, smiling at the shocked expression of the priest, "but a certain . . . disorderliness"—he savored the word, its delicious understatement: Targ thought he had just read too many books—"in his disposing of the body anytime, anywhere. There are many considerations. There are laws about such things. Regulations."

"He's dead. What does it matter to him?" Targ asked, gesturing toward the thing sheathed on the mattress. "He's dead. Leave it at that. Bury him in potter's field."

"Potter's field?"

"An American term. The cemetery for the poor. The civil cemetery."

"There is no such thing," the officer said. "They are all religious here, but not of *his* religion," he said, waving at the priest, his face turned toward the islander in the shadows. The priest glanced that way too, as if to intercept the line of the officer's gaze.

"Oh, but he must be buried," the priest said. "It is a matter of where. In most places, on the mainland, there is unconsecrated ground attached to cemeteries—you know, for the unbaptized, apostates, heretics, suicides, those killed in duels—or, on the other hand, any place of burial may be consecrated and thus constitute a valid, sanctified ground. We have no ground here . . . and yet he is, in a certain way, *ours,* even though he has placed himself outside the Church. He will always be ours. If land were set aside for us . . . for the unconsecrated dead . . ."

"That's not your decision. Only when *I* have released it can the body belong to you, even in consecrated ground. Please remember that."

The priest's accent was becoming better; he was dropping the vestiges of dialect as he kept talking. The phrase "placed himself outside the Church" had a grand ring to it. Targ could see the miserable old man taking his pills and saying, "Thus I place myself outside the Church," and doing it proudly with a grand gesture, striking some sort of absurd pose . . . a road-company Lucifer among his shabby effects. The priest's face had something of the actor about it: what was it? Too little head for too much face, permitting a mobile shifting from expression to expression, responding to needs, but masking, always, the sense of the missioned self beneath. Too many years of public pleading, acting, and prayer. It was almost as though he had merely assumed the islander's appearance in order to serve his Church better, or lead them. Selected effects for protective coloration.

"But he was the meekest man I knew," Targ said. No. Meek was not the right word. He *knew* that the old man had simply sat for a long while and thought. He hadn't been able to sleep. He felt alone. He waited for morning to come and realized that even though it would be daylight, he would still be old, alone in a world that had changed, and the loneliness was too much to bear. Yes, it probably happened that way. Nothing more. No point to make. And now, as so many literary critics and other interpreters of reality did, the gesture was being seized by reinterpretation. Targ could almost hear the priest saying, "But he sought Knowledge and thus committed an Act of Inordinate Pride." Targ knew the reasoning. And yet the young Trag in him almost nodded in agreement, not horrified but actually approving of grand gestures, horrified only at simple banal gestures inappropriate to grand moments.

The priest looked puzzled and shrugged his shoulders and said, "I'm sure he was." Meekness, for the priest, was not a category leading to action.

The officer looked suspiciously at the priest. "I know what you're trying to do."

"I suppose one of the islanders would be happy to sell some ground. You could bury him in such a plot, couldn't you?" Targ asked.

The officer again glanced quickly at the peasant islander.

Targ followed the look. Hands on knees; body stiff; back straight; legs short, almost not touching the floor; shadow-dappled face impassive (or unreadable to him). Was he young or old? An elder. It was always elders, wasn't it? Definitely an elder.

"No one can sell ground without the consent of all, their council, the community body, or, as they all put it, the totality," said the officer, glancing at the shadows. The statement was affirmative, definite; the tone was pitched as a question. "And rightly so. Impossible to convene at such a time of crisis. Even so, they would not bury him where they bury theirs, and their ground is everything but his" —he gestured at the priest—"ground."

"*My* ground? The Church's ground."

"Bury theirs? I thought the cemetery . . ."

"Oh, no. There are no islanders buried there. Isn't that true, Father?" The officer smirked. "They have their own places of burial."

"Then there's all that room in yours," Targ said to the priest.

"Yes," said the officer. "Precisely."

"Anyway, it's not my problem," Targ said.

"I told you, the Church cannot bury him," the priest said.

"Someone. Anyone," Targ said, annoyed. "Get it over with."

"The land of the Church cannot accept him."

"If it's not your problem, then why worry about it?" asked the officer. He had gone to the window and was peering over the shoulder of the suit, his hand on the shoulder. The gesture looked curiously like a comforting touch. "A place must be found, this problem solved. And soon."

"I can't even say prayers for him," the priest said.

Targ looked at the officer for his reply. The officer didn't say anything. Targ felt as if he was falling into a trapping routine: each statement and response, officer to priest, priest to officer, guided him, drew him into the debate, drew him along some path whose boundaries were the terms of the debate and whose destination he did not yet see. He tried to stop himself from saying anything. "I never said anything about prayer. I don't care about prayers. I'm talking about the body."

"But perhaps *he* does. . . ."

"*It* doesn't."

"Perhaps *he* cares about prayers now," the priest said, beginning to relish the idea.

"At any rate, anyone can bury the body," the officer said.

"Because to bury the body with rites is to admit him back to the community from which he has estranged himself," the priest said primly.

"If land could be bought."

"Murrr," said a spectral British voice, "Mord," or "Merde," or "Mare," or "Mary," or "Mord," or "Marred," or "Merde," or . . . It started faintly, came in closer, through the window, each sound emanating from another place as though someone invisible were teleporting in little leaps to some invisible point

among the three of them, and there stayed, repeating itself till it slowly faded into silence. At first the officer laughed at it, but seeming to remember something, sighed and looked young and puzzled for a second. He went to the window, looked out, and came back. "There's the sign."

The priest said, "I will never get used to it. I have experienced it for fifteen years now."

"A natural phenomenon," the officer said.

"The devil's voice. If I live here for the rest of my life"—he crossed himself—"I will not get used to this."

Targ looked at them.

"This superb phenomenon brings us voices from the sea," the officer explained pedantically. "Especially when everything becomes humid, just before the wet winds come. Something atmospheric and acoustical happens. Sometimes one hears the most interesting things said; the most interesting acts are committed, as on a stage. If they knew that these intimate moments . . ."

The priest put up his hand.

". . . these intimate businesses . . ."

The priest shook his finger.

"The tinkles of urination. Farts accompanying their defecations . . . Once we heard someone being tortured, on and off, for three days. The screams were unbelievable. Whoever it was was magnificent, denying . . . what shall I say? complicity? conspiracy? to the very end. I think they were using electrodes."

"Please . . ." the priest said.

The officer grinned and continued. ". . . their fornications; and that was not the worst: sodomy, group orgies, a regular Hieronymus Bosch *Walpurgis*—"

"Stop!" the priest thundered.

"All transmitted to us here all over the island, in a thousand places, sometimes cropping up between lovers in their very act or, as here, as if they were in the very room with us . . . or in church, out of the mouth or arse of our Saviour. It is a thing to look forward to," the officer said. "But it also means that the winds are on the way."

"It also means that," the priest said, shaking his head.

"Usually it takes place after the harvest is in. The festival is on. The peasants laugh and say it is the gods in their love, though it doesn't really translate that way since they don't have a word, or words, for god or gods. But now . . . now it is too early."

"The devil's voice. And can you understand what that means?" the priest said and crossed himself.

"How does one forget? One is racked with apprehension every harvest time. How does one forget?" They both went to the window and looked out over the suit's shoulders. Their bodies jostled and squeezed the suit. "It's really pointless to look. Nothing changes except in the smallest degree. And we can change nothing by our looking," the officer said.

"But we can pray."

"Prayer is pointless. We have to act. We have to do something. If these primitive idiots would only realize that the government would help them, and eagerly, when the crop fails; if they would only take that consolation and—"

"We *must* pray."

"I said act."

"Prayer is an act."

"And doing nothing is an act too. We cannot afford philosophical quibbles. Pray? It's nonsense. These are modern times. My country's good relief organization waits. Prayer, if you will, if you must. But organization ensures the prayer's answer."

"Don't blaspheme. Prayer and the answer to prayer alone developed *our* organization centuries ago."

"I am tired of this nonsense."

The priest crossed himself. The officer stuck his thumb between his first and second fingers and jiggled his hand upward twice. The priest clenched his fist and elevated his first and little fingers and jabbed. They were whispering fiercely across the front of the suit. The officer had the suit lapel in his fingers. They were into it smoothly now; the contention gave the sense of being staged. Targ felt irritable . . . as if they couldn't settle their differences till some purpose he could not detect was worked out. It was not his problem, not *his* play. Trag felt furious . . . as if they *wouldn't* settle their differences till some purpose, some price was worked out. It was becoming his problem; the contention was reviving feelings Targ had left behind so long ago. **And if the voice had really disappeared beneath the sheet, it reemerged again and was saying, quite precisely (except for the last word), "I tell you it is all murrrrr . . ." like a record running down.** Going over to the window was itself a form of conversation through gesture. But what were they *saying?* They came back to the center of the room. Six or seven flies rose from the sheet where they had been trying to get at the body.

"Something must be done, and quickly."

"A little land could be set aside . . ."

"But there are no public lands on this island . . . unless we count Church lands, which are, after all, quasipublic. To set any other land aside at a time like this is . . . dangerous."

"Doesn't your government have the power to . . . doesn't it own the land?" Targ asked. Why was he getting involved in this? Walk out. Let them settle it in their own way.

The priest smiled. "As they put it on this island, they don't own the land, the land owns them. That's of course not exactly it, but the sense of it. They have no word for property. Barbaric. But there *is* a system of ownership. A few years ago we had a few mathematical ethnologists here and they detected it, ownership cunningly hidden behind five or six layers of concealment . . . tenuous and subtle . . . a shadow of a tendency. It's extremely complicated and variable. . . . *You* might try talking to them."

"Me? It's not my problem," Targ said.

"You were his friend."

"I barely knew him. I'm not responsible," Targ told them.

"He's right. It's time a public place was made," the priest said. "We cannot have him, in spite of what he has done, like this. I don't approve of it, but it would solve so many problems."

"Yes, we must have land for the killed and the suicides. They are dropping like flies. We have so many to bury, don't we? Once a week, isn't it, that men are busy killing themselves here," the officer said.

"There's no need to be sarcastic."

"I see what your game is," the officer said. "And you expect me to broach such a topic as this, especially at this time, don't you? And how stupid do you think I am?"

"No. Really, old chap. We invest. Go long. Corner the futures. Get options on capacities and surpluses. . . ."

"Past futures?"

"Oh, that's good. That's really good."

"Fake futures?"

"That is even better. You're catching the spirit of it."

"Fake **past futures?"**

"Well, don't overdo it. We wait until it climbs. When it's high enough we dump, we dump, we dump. Glut the market. They lose faith. Prices plummet. We buy out again at a lower price and sell higher."

"But what if it drops while we have it? What if ***we're*** **buried? How long can we hold out?"**

"Don't worry. We can move it around. Keep selling it and reselling it. That will drive the price up too. It won't drop. Have no fear. It's a matter of chance, faith, timing, and time is with us. We have statistics, projections, reports, long- and short-term predictions. The seven fat years are over. World starvation is an unprecedented opportunity for growth. It's in the bag. We'll make a killing. Do you want to come in on it?"

"Stop it," Targ said.

". . . a fortune, I tell you."

"If they find out, there'll be a stink . . . an investigation."

"Then we buy the investigators. Don't worry. We can do whatever we want with the market: drive it up; drive it down."

"What if someone comes up with more . . . a hidden cache? Something we haven't taken account of? A new way of doing things?"

"Well, we can always sell to someone who's short. Someone's always short; pay big prices. You know, I think you're losing your balls."

The officer and the priest didn't seem to notice, or they accepted it. The officer said to Targ, "You see what an enormous mess your friend has made? You see how things are disrupted?"

You hear that? Targ thought at the sheet. Come back. There is no preparation for you. Start all over.

"But he must be buried. One cannot have him lying about like this," the priest said.

"Now *you're* in a hurry."

They stopped and looked at one another, come to an impasse. The suit hung limply; the wind had stopped blowing for a moment. They could hear the flies buzzing in the silence. They were waiting for him. Targ would say nothing.

A woman's light laugh drifted a little into the room, hovered for a second, and then faded away to be succeeded by the drip of water in a sink somewhere. Targ felt that he had heard that voice before. Helen from across the sea? No. "Really, what's the problem? It's so simple," Targ said.

"It is always simple for Americans," the officer said. "You are all famous for clearing away things. Poof, and you have resolved all troubles. Your famous bulldozer methods. But you never consider what a mess you create," he said, pointing at the body. "You haven't considered our position on this island."

"What does being American have to do with it?"

"It's a way of thinking. You have no respect for form and procedure. You don't think of the future. You have no respect for the way things should be done. It robs a man of dignity," the officer said. "Unless, of course, you *have* considered our position on this island."

Targ noticed the slight reversal, the use of the word "dignity." "What does that mean?"

"His act has upset delicate balances."

"If he's been robbed of dignity, he's robbed himself. What dignity can there be when you're dead?" Targ asked him. "There really is no pride to these things, only individual misery," he told the priest. "Anyway, what does that mean: your position on the island?" he said to the officer.

The officer shrugged. "Out there"—he gestured broadly—"is the American Sixth Fleet . . . the Russians . . . waiting . . ."

"That's ridiculous. I only met the man a few days ago." Dignity . . . that was what you accorded to friends and the great.

"There are ways of doing things," the officer said. "There are steps. Sequences." The officer had become rigid, standing at attention. He looked now, if anything, a little squatter, harder in his uniform. His chin jutted out, ready to defend procedure, the proper way of doing things; and since it was not murder, he was taking his resentment at the messy old man out on Targ. This willful man had upset everything; he had taken shortcuts. There was no way of handling such things because the officer had received no information about such contingencies and— He broke off in the middle and went to the window to emphasize what he was saying. His foot kicked the old man's cane; it fell; its nose broke off.

"He just wanted to be out of it," Targ told the policeman.

"But he had no right to do it that way," the priest said. "It's a terrible sin. It's a sign of despair."

"Shouldn't we despair? Aren't there reasons?" Targ asked. They looked at Targ, annoyed. "He did a simple thing. He was clearing the air."

"It will come too soon, I tell you," the priest muttered. "We must prepare. You see what has happened to us," he said to Targ. "God's punishment."

"Let's pretend that it never happened this way. Let's say that he died. Leave it at that. Then we could bury him," Targ said.

The priest looked at Targ, shocked. "Are you a Catholic?"

"No."

"Because you simply don't know what you're saying."

"Dead is dead. Bury him."

"I can understand the father's feelings," the officer said. "And dead is not dead but has ramifications that keep reaching out long after he is gone. Can you understand, for instance, that on the night of your arrival I made an entry into the day's report?"

"So?"

" 'So'? What do you mean, 'so'? There are entries before and entries after the event. A man does not simply disappear. There is also a corresponding space into which I must write the time of departure. He must be accounted for. Therefore a man does not cease to be."

"He did," Targ said and smiled.

"It is not funny. A man shouldn't set himself up against the way things are."

Old hero, Targ thought, old iconoclast, smashing himself utterly and bringing them fluttering around the room with their "what is to be done" cluckings.

"Slut," a hoarse, brutal Italian voice said. "Slut. You don't care who sticks it into you, do you?"

"Who do you think you're talking to? Who? Call *me* a slut?" a woman's beautiful voice sopranoed gently, as though singing a lullaby.

"Slut," grated the man's voice. It was a South Italian dialect. "Go. Put it into any bed. Lay it down for anyone. I should throw you off the boat."

"Throw," her Tuscan voice said. "Go ahead. Throw."

Targ laughed and laughed.

"This is nothing to laugh about. The devil's diversion," the priest said.

Targ looked at the sheet. He waved his hand over it. Flies rose again into the now sticky air. "Some hero," Targ told them.

"How can you call him a hero . . . a man who will do a thing like that . . . a Catholic?"

Targ saw that the priest, after all, was merely a working priest, a man without imagination. He had hoped for subtleties, but that was more the fault of too much contact with academics and books. In literature priests were subtle, they made long, reflective speeches, balancing a multiplicity of nuances, and talked about "the human condition." In life this priest was disgusted, preoccupied, a little stupid, reflexively thinking of Kairos as a great sinner; completely unconcerned with shades of heroism, concerned only with the oncoming weather, compulsively spiteful to the officer, determined to keep his cemetery untarnished, perhaps even to extend the Church's holdings by having auxiliary lands set aside for the "sinners," preserving, extending his position, half superstitious about the body and avoiding of it. And if he were to have a discussion with the priest about the meaning of the Middle Ages, what would the man say, or care? Targ remembered old quarrels with the literary and political Jesuits of the university; after all, there was more than a little of the actor about them all. It also took actors to keep the world running. It was just that he and they now came from different schools of theater. . . . Philidor, who wasn't even a Catholic, knew much more about it than this priest did. But then this man wasn't even a university teacher and so didn't care about that gone, that perfect, that universal and structured time when everything was supposed to be arranged and accounted for in perfect hierarchies. They did not send Aquini or Loyoli to places like these. And yet it didn't matter whom they sent. They sent modes of procedure disguised as people. Sophisticated or crude, they shared one attribute, which was to give up not one thing, not one element of their vast constructs, constructs which came from outside themselves completely, constructs to which they were connected as if their nervous systems, their blood networks, their hormonal ethers went beyond the skins of their bodies; constructs which, sustained by thousands who in turn acted on millions, replaced themselves constantly by a process of selection, selection of those who had an affinity (one might even say a genetic affinity) for acting out these grand dramas; selection, out of sets of possible psychotypes, of those who were the fittest to ensure the survival of these constructs and became themselves elements linked into strings and networks. . . .

But he was out of it now. He had seen too much. He had . . . broken down, seen that the strings and networks and arrangements of events were acts of massed wills, and those wills not the ultimate desires of actors, motivators, conduits, particles. . . .

But then you see, thought Trag, how this magnificent act—

Magnificent? What? Taking poison?

Existential . . . Trag giggled. He felt just like a schoolboy again, ready for all kinds of pranks. He understood the priest and the officer now, understood their impasse.

He had met them before, had Trag, these metal men. He knew them, he knew them, knew their advents, their rises to power, their long years of reign, their declines. They were stamped-out emanations of power; icons who thought they were alive. He had met them a thousand times in every history book and in a thousand dreams, met them in high university councils. He had seen Targ become one of them when he had stopped being Trag. Targ had reinforced his position during the Great Student Rebellions, known the joy of being ruthless, discarding the past, using the rebellion to get rid, once and for all, of the dead wood of the past, known the joy of evolving plans and fighting, maneuvering first with the rebellious students and the meta-university revolutionists, getting those plans implemented over the obstacles of reflexive men of limited vision hanging onto the wrong past. So he knew the priest and the officer and how to deal with them. They were handling the problem by defining it, isolating it, encapsulating it, excising it, removing it . . . and preserving it. It was no longer necessary for Targ even to listen to their words, which would, with variations, be repeated over and over again. But his mind was dulled; he was hungry and tired; all he could do was watch their positions, observe the way they changed, see gestures and hear only the tones . . . till it became abstracted for him into a pure positional play danced over the body of Kairos, each movement being a repetition with variations of what they had said before.

And yet there was another element, whose presence and nature were not yet clear. Himself. They argued for him: *he* was the audience, and that troubled him. The island elder sat in the shadows and Targ wasn't even sure he spoke the language. The islander didn't matter. It was not Targ's problem. Tiredness, hunger, petulance, annoyance, a lack of belief, anxiety made Targ irritable because he was unable to sleep. And yet it was his problem, for the puzzle of the game intrigued him. A reflex from the past. And he could see that the very sustaining of the argument, its persistence, its boring unresolvability, made him part of it and channeled *him* to participate in the resolution, which he couldn't foresee. There was only one way to retaliate: Targ must get them to resolve their differences and bury Kairos. Targ began to think it out. Be cold. Be dispassionate. Calculate it. He wished he had Helen here to help him, as she always had. But then he reminded himself that he had done it well before there was even such a thing as a Helen. He began to feel a little better, but not enough yet. He assessed. Who should represent you, old body, my body, nobody knows. . . . The islander rubbed his nose with the side of a thick forefinger. It was Cyclops' daughter: a trick of light . . . and lingering desire. He began: "Listen, it's only flesh, which is to say a concourse and conglomerate of molecules united into a something that is . . . was, really, more than the sum of constituent molecules. The binding power is . . . no, *was* . . . what? Magnetism? Magnetohumanity, life, will? Which is the process of being a human . . . this 'between-state.' "

"The soul . . ." the priest said.

"Soul . . ." the officer sneered.

"But that's over with. Yet you both persist in keeping that now-gone state going after death. You set against one another two variations of resurrection. . . . You needn't shake your head," he said to the officer. ". . . a traffic in dead souls, or persistent symbols representing, and preventing from dissolving, this conglomerate of particles. But it doesn't matter, least of all to the *no longer him,* who, I am sure, forgot his Catholicism or, on the other hand, his official place in the grand continuity of paper work thousands of years ago. Didn't you, old body?" Targ asked of the sheet.

Trag screamed at him, screamed at the playful irony, the deadness of the words, at the inhumanity, at the calmness and callousness, at the humorousness of the tone. The scream merged into the alarm siren of a warship signaling condition red, counterpointed by a panting, wordless voice coming and carried through the humid air, hanging there, pulsating, hot with excitement and torment. Targ couldn't tell if it was a woman's or a man's voice, but how crude to fuck in the presence of the dead.

Their poses were broken; their hands were held to their ears, their faces contorted: they waited for the sound to abate. Only the islander sat unmoving, immobile as a statue, sitting on terrific pedestals, blind eyes overseeing thousands of years of pleas. That was why the pedestal in the temple was empty. The sound gradually lessened, softened, but persisted, rising and falling, the highs and lows merging till it diminished into an ever ready hum.

Trag, he thought, had always been such a romantic, a heaven stormer, an overreacher, so easy to outrage.

The officer smiled. Targ had been right about his commitment to the rational world. The priest, horrified, or acting out a horrified ritual, crossed himself and said, "Mother of God." And so he saw that the smile was itself a ritual gesture to evoke the exclamation.

"So it will make things easier for us to take the body, slice it down to slivers, strew the parts all over the fields so as to give the earth more fertility. I'm sure, no matter what emotional words you attach to this act, you and the islanders can agree on these common principles," he said to the priest, "since you all share some theory of sacrifices and fertility." Targ smiled directly at the islander who sat in the shadows. "Mark it buried in your records or, for that matter, transfer it to your agricultural records," he said to the officer. "Leave it at that," he said to them both.

"You cannot do a thing like that," the officer said. "Now, if some land were set aside . . ." and they were off again, arguing bitterly about it, both admitting death but not the dissolution of the personality and responsibility even after ultimate decomposition into particles, one compelled to treat the body as a great sinner, the other talking of the body as if it still retained some great anarchical power to destroy the logic of his forms.

Targ shrugged. It was pointless. He gave up. He began to yawn. "Can I get some food somewhere?" he asked. Targ walked over to the body and lifted a corner of the sheet. "You've brought them to an impasse," he said to the dead but staring face. The tongue protruded out of the mouth corner, the eyes were crossed, the forelock of hair stuck straight up. A fly came down. Targ brushed it away and closed the sheet. They were silent suddenly, looking at Targ. Why had he done that? He had forgotten what the face looked like.

"How can you treat the dead that way?" the priest asked.

"I didn't notice you treating death any better."

"He's still a human being . . ." the officer started to say and stopped when he looked at Targ's grin. "You're not behaving well."

"Stinks. Decomposing. Hurry. Freeze it. Spice it. Do something. It stinks."

They pretended to smell nothing. They resumed their arguments. Their tones had become completely flat now, had degenerated into pure style and repetition as if they both accepted the fact that the passion behind their arguments was no longer necessary to voice and yet they must merely repeat. Targ yawned. The yawn, a mighty one, shook his whole body and distorted his vision as his eyeballs were squeezed. His ears popped and he heard a rush of waters which was the sound of pulse in his head. In that moment Targ noticed that their arguments were made as presentation to the simple islander who sat in shadows. The distortion of his vision showed him peasant elder and Cyclops' daughter sitting vast, naked, timeless there, her great body gross, her breasts vaster than he remembered them. And yet her face was young, innocent as a child's, but her belly, thighs, and crotch were used, wise, knowledgeable. So now he saw (what did it matter, after all?) that what the officer said and what the priest said mattered and didn't matter. For yes, for a second he could have sworn that they were united to that darkness, clumping/diffusing in the representation of a person stirring in the shadow. He resisted giving it a face, a body, resisted resolving or coalescing those shadows into idols, drawings, statues, icons, photographs, gods, printouts, goddesses—any of the representations of forces of the past—preferring to think of those shadows as . . . what? A background . . . out of which came volition. And his very tiredness helped to sustain this insight. And that's why the designations and costumes and customs and masks and masques called officer fighting with priest were false. *They were islanders.* Two aspects of a multiple entity in contention against him were, after all, *not* men of power in the way he usually thought of them at all. His primary evaluation had been wrong. Knowing this now, he stored the knowledge for future use, for it was a delicate matter, tenuous and possibly not even usable. And now Targ understood, though he must not admit it, that they had succeeded in allying him with the corpse. And he began to fear. The yawn ended. He stared directly. He saw nothing out of the ordinary. The old islander, perhaps an elder, was still smiling slightly. He glanced away and peered with his peripheral vision. Furious movement? Almost. Nothing.

Targ went out, leaving them all walking back and forth from the body to the window. The pulsating voice hum followed him down the corridor to his room, but stopped at his door. He remembered he had forgotten his suitcase. He went back. They were gone. When he brought his suitcase to his room, the priest and the officer were in his room.

The officer was sitting at the head of Targ's bed; the priest was standing by the chest of drawers, his hands on the surface, sliding them back and forth. The priest's face was calm and smooth. The policeman looked contented. He had just done something clever. "After long deliberations, much soul searching and debate, we have come to a decision," the officer said.

Targ shrugged. "Good."

"It's not a decision that pleases one. There is nothing else to do. There was nothing else to do from the beginning."

It seemed to have happened with surprising speed. He was too tired to ask. He sat down beside the policeman, bent down and began to unlace his sneakers, to introduce a little dissonance into their plans. He acted more tired than he was in order to avoid setting up resistances by any act of his.

"To review: There is no land for the body, religious or secular or private. We have spoken with the council, the body, and gotten nowhere. You have no idea how superstitious these people are. In fact, they cannot even recognize the very idea of suicide . . . their language has no such concept."

When had they had the time to speak with the body, or the totality, whatever it was? Targ lay down on his back.

"They feel it would be catastrophic. In fact, these savages say that they now understand the real causes of the unseasonal arrival of the seasonal winds. I tried to explain, in scientific terms, change of prevailing wind patterns, interglacials . . . I won't go into it all. There is no land available."

"We have decided," the priest intoned. Targ lifted his head and saw, sleepily, the priest standing there, quite close to his feet, towering now, black in his robes . . . because of the way the light fell, of course.

Targ could feel the bed shake as the officer changed his position and shrugged. "Therefore it is a question of what *you* must do."

They were silent. Targ started to drift off and fall asleep. The officer shifted again and said, "The man came from America; let him be returned to rest there."

"Good enough," Targ murmured.

"*You* will take the body. . . ."

"Who? Targ?" Trag asked the voice, which came from a long way off.

"You."

Targ turned away and lay on his side and put his arm under his head. "Hire somebody," he told his elbow.

"No man on this island will touch the body, an outsider and a suicide to boot," the priest said; he had come around to the side and knelt down so that his face was only a few inches from Targ's.

"With all due respect to your beliefs, Father; but we're all educated men here, even him." Targ pointed with his thumb behind him, toward the officer, but meaning Kairos in the next room. "And I'm sure that even the Church has some brand-new encyclicals about it . . ."

"I haven't received any."

". . . because, after all, the fathers realize that this is the twentieth century and there is no longer the importance attached to—"

The officer leaned over Targ's head. "It is pointless to argue," he said and his mind was made up. Out of the corner of his eye Targ saw that the officer's face was brazen, fixed now in the flickering candlelight; unmoved, not even **hearing the grand polonaise that poured into Targ's room, echoing in the room as if in the inside of an enormous deserted ballroom.** They remained, their faces close to his, the priest's in front of Targ's, the officer's bent close to Targ's ear.

Targ resented it. Their breaths were bad. He closed Targ's eyes. He hated the stupidity of it all. He hated the incredible bother that would be involved. He tried to try and sleep; he could hear their heavy breathing. But beneath his shell of calmness and weariness, even of disinterest, some nonheart pulse oscillated much faster and more irregularly than his cardiac pulse. It was the difference between the subbeat and his regular pulse that was making him panicky.

He would, thought Trag, but not now . . . he would surprise them all. He listened with closed eyes in order to hear better: his face in repose would mask his thoughts.

Trag opened his eyes. "I won't do it," he said. And felt the hatred, like regurgitant stomach juices, rumble in his body, sweep up till he could taste the distaste of it in his mouth. "I won't do it," he belched and the priest moved back.

The officer became still squatter, still harder (Targ felt, and interpreted the movement on the bed even if he couldn't see a change of position), revealing his island nature. Targ knew it was the wrong thing to say; it was done too quickly, but he couldn't help himself: he wanted to sleep so badly. The officer smiled a little. Targ understood that every opposition would simply add to the officer's happy stubbornness: a joy at having the monotony of his existence change a little. What, Targ wondered, had that old fool got him into? No. Kairos wasn't a hero, a Lucifer choosing his despair, a destroyer of the neat and planned forms of life; he was a nuisance, an about-to-stink piece of meat who had, while alive, been monstrously inconsiderate out of some mawkish self-pity. . . . After all, Targ thought, "despair" or "spiritual crisis": these were really concepts too grand to apply to this little misdemeanor. Targ turned and looked up into the officer's face. He recognized the look. They seized whatever fugitive tide-moment came along and rode it, thinking they were controlling it, even in opposition to it, sometimes that they had originated it. So Targ knew how to handle these jokers whose fiats could only chain him to the dead joker's body. Of course, he could have said, "All right. I didn't want to tell you. He was killed."

"Who killed him?"

"One of the islanders." But that was silly on the face of it. So Targ would then have to say, as if making an admission reluctantly: "I killed him." That would permit them to bury Kairos. But that was silly too. What motive had he had? "Because he was annoying," Targ thought.

"Annoying? Come now."

"A fit of pique," Targ thought.

"One could kill, but hardly for that," was the answer.

"If one can kill, one can kill for any reason."

"You're only trying to shirk your responsibility."

His defense collapsed. He would have to try another way.

The priest stood up, looking disgusted, turned away, and walked back toward the chest of drawers, lifting his head and hands as if called upon to make some comment to the Great Auditor.

"Cold meat," Targ mocked. "No more. Don't dignify it by complications. . . . Bury the dead." Targ yawned.

"As you say," the officer said, but now he looked a little disturbed. "But this man was, after all, your friend. Someone must escort the body to the mainland. It's only fit."

"Yes, he was my friend," Trag said. A friend deserved better than this.

Targ sat up, leaned forward, propped his hands on his knees, his chin in his hands. "That's your outlook. It's bad enough I'm stuck here for another few days. You're only palming off your responsibilities on me."

"No. It *is* your outlook," the officer insisted.

"He's nothing to me," Targ said.

"He's an American."

"He's a human being," said the priest.

"I really doubt that."

"Why do you say that?"

"The way he shrugged his shoulders."

"Really . . ."

"No American shrugs his shoulders that way."

"Really . . ."

"And even so, I'm not responsible for every American."

"Be reasonable. It's only a matter of bringing . . . escorting the body to the mainland. You won't even have to touch it. Then you'll be free."

"I don't want to get involved with it."

"Are you superstitious?"

"No; I want out. I don't want the bother."

"What bother? You merely go on the same boat. When you get

there you simply inform the police, the consulate, and then, of course, they take over and do the rest. I will send a report with you."

Something loose in Targ's head jarred and beat and he thought: I am being foolish. He turned toward the officer and propped himself up on his hand. At most it would only entail a wasted day, no more than two. What did he have to do with his time anyway? But he could see what would, what must happen. The ferry would come. Helen would surely be on it. He would have to explain it all to her. He would have to answer the questions she would ask. Then there would be the long, the boring, the stupid day spent on the island, anticipating what would happen, trying not to think about it, being forced to remember Kairos, moving around in this thickening, sticky, enervating air. Then there would be the trip back. And then, again, explanations to the mainland police. That inevitable going through a long series of questions and subquestions and answers, qualified answers, modified answers to fit the filling out of their inevitable and interminable forms, explanations to various policemen embedded in their positions in the galling bureaucracy. And of course they would have to try out their policemen's tricks; these questions they always *had* to ask, with implications that Targ had done it . . . that *had* to follow. And then the consulate.

But what if the officer was really convinced it *was* murder and was using this as a means of delivering him into the hands of the mainland police? Hadn't he accepted the fact of suicide too easily? None of the Javert in him; that was suspicious. Had there really been enough investigation? What if the poison had been forced on Kairos? After all, it shouldn't have been too hard; he was an old man. But then why hadn't he simply arrested Targ? Ahhh . . . Targ thought, the coming crisis. The weather and the crops. The islanders burning . . . He remembered Kairos and the fire-catching tip of his cane. What could he do to prevent Targ from delivering the body to the mainland in person?

Then who knew; once delivered, they might consider the whole question in the realm of health . . . a potential disease-bearing source, requiring quarantine. Therefore, a something to be sent away because it was threatening. Were there rules against the importation of certain products? Insects? Poisons? Plants? Viruses? Contaminant genetic material? Animals dangerous to native crops? Sacrificial contaminants? Debilitating customs? Under which category was Kairos?

Now, suppose all explanations were accepted. Even so, once a process had been initiated, there was no way of stopping it. Therefore, probably, they wouldn't even allow Kairos to be buried on the mainland. The thing hadn't been sent to them for final resolution, but rather for administrative and jurisdictional disposal and processing. And then they would say to Targ, "What now?" and he would have to take Kairos home. That would spoil his vacation because it was too soon to return home yet. Thus they would be forced to convey Kairos wherever they went. To be sure, modern techniques would enable them to have the coffin completely sealed . . . plastic and caulking, perhaps, could do the job. Refrigeration. But that would cost them for the extra baggage and would delay them interminably at every frontier. Would they slap travel stickers on it to show where it had been? It would look festive that way. Keep moving with the body, from country to country; more explanations, till an enormous dossier had been built up . . . eventually to the United States.

And all Kairos really had wanted was to remain here . . . to belong. Had Targ told them that? Tell them. Flatter them. It wouldn't matter.

He foresaw all this and it made him furious: furious at the priest, furious at the officer, furious at the natives; furious at Helen; furious at the chancellor; furious at the university; furious at Professor Biddle; furious at himself; furious at Trag nagging at him.

The officer stood up. "Really," he said. "I don't see why you are making so much of it. A small inconvenience . . . no more."

All Targ could say, spitefully, was, "You can't allow him to lie there like that till it's time to go. He's beginning to stink." And he turned away from them and closed his eyes. He was almost asleep instantly and heard them, vaguely, leave. And when they were gone he would sleep . . . until another plan would form.

11

But Targ's body finally went to sleep, if only because lulled by the unchanging monotony of his room. He had been kept awake by the thinking about, the getting exasperated by the process, every step he would have to go through. He fretted dismally, petulantly at each adamant barrier and each marble official face that must confront him . . . a long, perhaps unending series of people in many countries who would lock him tighter and tighter to the body. He could already see them; he had talks with them; the discussions were interminable. Snatches of dialogue, some of them quite brilliant, were played out in his mind, where, by the force of sheer reason and logic, he demonstrated why the body was not his problem. Then, taking the part of an official, he would answer even more brilliantly, but it had nothing to do with reason or logic but something else. Stalemate. Now and then he would get exasperated and begin to rage, the untamed Trag in him taking over, becoming a vicious and sarcastic third. Other times he would, in pleading, in explaining, tell them about Kairos, building up his life, giving him a rich past which he constructed from the few clues Kairos had passed on to him.

He woke for a second from a dream in which Helen mounted Kairos, who kept, always, that antic death pose.

"Get away from that. It's mine," Targ said.

She grasped his forelock like a rein and began to ride him, moving herself up and down.

"He's dead, you know," Targ remarked to her.

"I'll bring him to life."

"You don't have to do *this* for me."

"I'm not, my love," she said. "But one must appease the faculty somehow. *We're* doing this for you, for us. We'll bring ourselves out of it yet."

"But I don't want to get there."

"It's too late. You're committed. I know the secret of how you changed your name," she said.

"But I did it for you."

She laughed.

And he had to watch them doing this sexual act. Suddenly, still impaled, she flipped herself over, whirling Kairos. Now the old man crabbed on top of her, all rigid. She, mobile and fluid, embraced him and bounced him. It was embarrassing to Targ, especially when they began to smell of sex, or decomposition; he didn't know which: both. As they kept fucking, the rhythm and vibration of the act (that and an advanced state of death) began to shake Kairos apart. Targ was amused by this. Helen grinned, became frantic, and doubled the speed of the rhythm of her movements, as if she had to finish before

Kairos had fallen apart entirely. The speeded-up motion increased the rate of dissolution. Her panicked hands kept reaching around her to grab pieces of Kairos. She tried to stick them back onto the body, not caring where she stuck them. Slowly, slowly, Kairos was being sucked into her. He fell apart faster than she could put him together again. She adapted. Her feet became prehensile, like hands. Her elbow and knee joints dissolved and her arms and legs were loose and fluid, practical and undulant. Kairos began to dissolve into liquid faster than she could ingest him. She adjusted: her many limbs now had suckers on the ends of them to slurp up the viscid liquid. Her pants and cries of joyandpain were now regular, deep, mechanical like a pump. She sent down limbs to the floor to anchor her and give her better balance. Finger and rake points clawed the wood; plant tendrils sank below the surface; nails splintered the wood; bolts and screws sustained the heaving body on the bed; a breast elongated and ended in nylon piping; wires trailed. . . . Parts of her body continued to shrink, disappear; other parts shifted; her cunt had grown enormous and was now edged with the thick, luxurious blond head hair; she was becoming wholly specialized in the emergency. Kairos was being sucked in faster now.

"Oh, no you don't," screamed Trag, and he jumped to the side of the bed.

"Stay back, you stupid fool," said Targ. "She's only hiding the body so we can get off this stupid island."

But Trag grabbed pieces of Kairos and began to pull.

Soft lips on a vine climbed to meet Trag's lips. Trag turned his face away. Her motherly mouth sought the flesh behind his ear; teeth bit his lobe softly. A tennis arm held his waist and a strong hand caressed and squeezed his buttock while a breast inserted itself into his hand.

"She always wanted to be a mother," Targ said. But he became jealous and turned his back on the whole thing. He went to sleep again and woke and thought he still heard the fugitive sounds of a mating in the next room, but obviously it had been transmitted to him through the humid air from one of the boats. He thought he recognized the woman's voice. When had he heard it before? And, as always, it was so real that he thought his dream was real too. Confused, he wondered if the people on the boats heard what was happening to him as well as he heard them. He had to light the candle. There was no one there. The sounds cut off suddenly at the light. He was sweaty and hungry.

It was an early foggy morning. His window seemed to be made of yellow sheeting. Nothing was visible through it but an eternal yellow haze which held suspended in it the eternal smells of the various and futile manures. When Targ looked out, he could barely see the sea. All the sharp contrasts which constituted a usual sunny Mediterranean day were not there at all. The haze had caught the rays of the sun and diffused them evenly.

Because of the opacity of the air, Targ could see his own image in the window's glass. He hovered vaguely over the faint sea, superimposed on a few very near pleasure boats which cut through the greenish water, leaving their small and oily wakes. They were closer to the shore than he remembered them being before. Targ looked unshaven; his hair was disarrayed and pasted into recalcitrant knots down over his forehead; his face was gaunt. The white shirt he had worn was creased into thousands of little folds and the collar ends, which had somehow become unbuttoned in the night, were twisted up and away. Targ lit a cigarette, watched the smoke rise, welcomed the smell of it. He looked down at his pants. They were crumpled and the wrinkles lifted the cuffs clear of his ankles. Targ changed his shirt but didn't bother with the pants; it was too much trouble. He remembered his dream and Kairos's body in the next room and the pointless, irritating stupidity that he would have to go through. No. He had decided. He went out.

Targ passed the open door of the old man's room. The bed was empty. They had removed the body. Where had they put it?

Targ went downstairs. No one was left in the streets. They were probably all in the fields now, working furiously to finish the harvest before the wind came and ruined it all. Targ went to the café and knocked on the door. No one answered. There was no one at the police station. Targ started to walk out of town and passed the church; the doors were locked. They were all in the fields. Targ went back to wait for the ferry to come; there was nothing else to do. He didn't know what time it was. He hadn't rewound his watch. Its hands showed some obsolete hour. Targ wandered. He wondered if even she, the three-eyed woman, had been asked to help with the harvest.

After a long while the haze-embedded source of light had shifted itself a little till it seemed to be beyond the meridian. Targ heard a boat whistle sounding. Resounding echoes came down off the hill. For a second, from far out, it looked like a pleasure boat was trying to come in. Targ walked down to the wharf and passed the warehouse. He stopped and rattled the warehouse door. The latch was held together with a combination lock; the latch itself was set in half-rotten warped wood. Targ remembered reading once that when the dial was turned, each significant number revealed itself by a little click of tumblers in the lock. Targ bent down and put his ear to the lock and began to turn. But when he adjusted himself to this new position, hunger made his stomach wail and rumble and prevented him from hearing anything. He tasted something bitter. The sudden smell of the rancid sea, coming up through the wharf planks, made his head reel. He had to stand up and lean against the wall of the warehouse till he caught his breath and the dizziness stopped. Targ tried to listen for the tumblers again, but the raucous cries of the sea gulls, the slap of the waves on the pilings, which slightly shook the whole wharf and warehouse, the roar of the tide on the beach, the long-drawn-out hiss of the receding waters, the noise of wind strumming some taut boards . . . all prevented his hearing anything. Everything was definitely against him.

He walked to the end of the wharf and looked at the ferry. It was nearer, but still a long way off. The diffused haze of skywater reddened as the sun began to go down. Targ walked back to the land end of the wharf. He walked up and down, getting hungrier and a little more nauseated. The mainland was quite invisible. Targ heard the sound of strong and steady diesels churning. It wasn't the ferry's motor. Naval boats? He passed the warehouse two or three times. He looked in.

The window was dusty, crusted, almost impossible to see through. Targ couldn't be sure of what he saw at first: it was a dust-pointillist portrait out of which to construct reality. A long, low hall, dim and dark, seemed to stretch away for a greater distance than the outside length. Perhaps that was because of the distorting powers of the dustiness, which in itself was a sort of lens, or anti-lens. The sloped roof pointed up into darkness; beams were suspended from the darkness. Nets, ropes, chains, a traveling crane hung from the beams. Targ saw something thick and heavy, like a warped bale, or a great stone, or a pillar, or yes, a pale canvas sack, half propped against something, half on the floor. It was tied haphazardly all over with black ropes.

They had put Kairos there. Targ was sure of it. They had carelessly thrown the body in, letting it rest however it had fallen. It leaned precariously (making Targ catch his breath), comically—if one considered what was in it—about to fall, held in place only by the body's death-stiffness. Targ looked away and out to sea. The ferry had come in a little nearer. He could almost see people. He wondered if she was on it. Targ smelled something stronger than the salt smell of the sea, stronger than the smell of the rotting seaweed, stronger than the ubiquitous smell of animal urine and droppings. He was sure it was the smell (though he had never smelled it before) of a decomposing body. It was strong enough to overcome everything else, to come through the sack and through the warehouse walls. Stop being silly, Targ thought. It was ridiculous to think that the smell could possibly be so strong yet. After all, Targ thought, he had killed himself only yesterday. He was surprised to think it; it seemed so long ago.

Targ went away from there quickly. He went to the edge of the wharf. He stood there watching the boat coming closer and closer. It manufactured itself through the haze. Then it seemed to disappear for a second and he blinked, and then the ferry was coming again, but somehow off to the side of its previous wake. He could hear the pound and throb of the old engine. The motor cut off. He heard the hiss of the long glide in. Targ thought he saw Helen standing in the prow, looking cool and slim. She seemed dressed in a white-and-blue-striped jacket made out of cotton, which blew back in the breeze like wings. Her blond hair was tied into a long and tossing tail, held together with a silver clip. Her face was clean and shining, almost blazing with light. She watched the island. She peered . . . obviously for Targ. Didn't she see him? She worried a little—he knew the signs—but she was still, as always, cool, sensible, able to act. You've saved me so many times, Targ thought, but what can you do for Targ now? The boat came closer and she *was* there, standing in the prow as Targ had always imagined her: clean, beautiful, and, to be sure, quite without smell; however, the wind did not wing her jacket. She didn't wave but kept looking toward the wharf, toward the land, toward the high green domed hill as the boat whistled one last time.

One of the sailors threw the weighted rope high into the air, hopped down to the wharf, caught the rope, and began to warp the boat in. Her eyes scanned around, passed Targ, went on, looked anxiously up the street. . . . Then she realized she *had* seen Targ; she smiled and waved. Targ could see the momentary bewilderment; her face asked, but her voice would not address questions to Targ. She must only accept him as he was and always waited for him to speak first and set the rules of discourse. It was her role. For she treated all his actions as psychological aberration, Targ thought, which enabled her to be loving, forgiving, even of the arms of other women . . . any cruelty offered her. After all, didn't he forgive her the arms of Kairos? No, no. He forgot. It was only a dream. But he could feel very old angers settling down around him because he wanted to feel (though he knew it not to be so) that the whole misadventure was somehow her fault. That it was a trap.

When they put down the gangplank, she came down, carrying her suitcase and managing to move with ease despite her white high-heeled shoes, doing it as she did all simple acts, superbly. Perhaps there was hope; all nonsense must stop in the face of someone as palpably healthy and sensible as she was. She would manage to set it right. She would explain how it had all happened. The whole thing had been another one of his self-torturing whims, another fantasy evoked to make life interesting, multi-evented, to hurt them both so he could feel. There was no old man who had undergone a spiritual crisis. No old man who challenged heaven's way with his despair, who selfishly apportioned his living self to nothingness. No old man who disrupted the smooth conditioned flow of ancient bureaucratic procedure and ancient harvesting customs and rituals. He had not (in spite of the fact that he must pay for it for the rest of eternity) challenged all and taken a chance. And he had not stood against the neat and tedious arrangements of that poetic bureaucrat, that prosaic priest, that superstitious islander and made a mess that called for such an expedient and inadequate solution. Kairos had not committed suicide.

Had Targ's face revealed something? Targ caught that little look that showed Helen was determined to *accept,* not to question, to be Christian, to be loving. This time she was reading him wrong. So Targ said nothing to her at all. And she, in turn, forbore from asking those million questions she should ask. Targ thought: We'll see who will weaken first. She answered by embracing and kissing Targ, dirt or no dirt. He noticed that her hair had become suddenly dank and limp in the damp, enchanted air.

Targ picked up her suitcase and started to walk. She linked her hand in Targ's free arm and walked along. The white of her glove was whiter than the white of his shirt. He slid his hand back and took her hand and squeezed, smudging her glove; he felt better, even affectionate. Targ saw that the sailors had all left, going ahead of them up the wharf and street, looking anxiously, from time to time, at the hazy sky, toward the way from which the wild wet wind would come. Targ wondered if they were going to help with the harvest. As he passed the warehouse, he left Helen for a second to look through the window. The sack was still in that ludicrous position, about to fall, and Targ felt like laughing. "Well, you were a long time," Targ told her. "Was Paris helpful?"

She laughed. "The things they have for women. The things they dream up. Do you like me?" she said and stepped away, pirouetting her white pleated skirt out from her long bronze legs; freezing as in a stop-time commercial, moving, flaring out her vertically striped blue-and-white little jacket so that it looked like wings; freezing (and he froze with her), holding her arms wide so that the hollow under where her pectoral and arm muscles joined showed. Her unbound breasts bounced under the damp striping of her sleeveless blouse; she swirled; stopped, and the island itself, arrested, jarred, and he almost fell. A strand of coral circled her brown neck.

"I like you," Targ told her but felt new differences between them. It could only anger Trag. *Anything* she did could only anger Trag.

"I met some people with a yacht while I was waiting for you. A converted destroyer. Endless space, beds, op-art awnings, drinks, little cans of delicacies, narcotics . . . They've invited us to go along: a cruise. He's one of those tanker Greeks. And she . . . well, there are in fact many shes, not necessarily men or women. He's one of those self-educated types, like Mr. Kairos, risen from the slums to the top of the world of business. From Piraeus to Parthenon in one generation, as he puts it. Of course, he's an art lover and a collector . . . you know the type. He says he plays Alexander to so many Aristotles . . . and laughs and laughs. He thinks that no American can understand Greece, so he'd like a debate. They're cruising the Mediterranean. Would you like that?"

"Why not?" Targ asked calmly. He felt like laughing; the sense of relief was too much. Now they could take Kairos and bury him at sea. He would be able to divest himself of the body now. . . .

"All kinds of people come and go, night and day; businessmen arrive by helicopter and boat. Scholars with rare specialties . . . He had a terrific fight with an Arabic Aristotelian. . . . He just loved the idea of your interest in relics . . . *his* relics, he calls them, since he is, as he puts it, a true Athenian. He speaks English with a slum Greco-Oxford accent that he learned very carefully. They want to see the naval exercises first. A big mock battle staged near this island. Thousands of men landing. A spectacular. Almost as big as *The Longest Day.* Russians, Americans, NATO . . . I don't know what else. He even has some film makers along who will shoot footage for a movie they're making, even though it has nothing to do with the sea."

"Why not?" The body would have to remain in that position a little bit longer, but that couldn't be helped.

"And there's going to be a famous actor and his wife and/or mistress and boyfriend—I'm not sure which is which. I think some degenerated nobility à la Proust. *We* will represent stability," she said and laughed gaily. "Isn't that wild?"

"That sounds nice enough," Targ said and saw she knew he meant that sounded horrible; but at least they would get Targ away from here and away from that corpse.

"But I don't think their invitation includes your friend. How is dear Mr. Kairos, by the way?" And she couldn't help looking at Targ as if to say: Don't be difficult; don't be spiteful. It would be amusing, Targ thought, to have *his* voice coming to the island out of the nothingness, even as they might be standing there and wondering where he had gone to. Targ thought again of that stiffened sack.

"Actually they might like him, because he's dead. Maybe *that's* missing from their menagerie," Targ said and watched her carefully to see if she broke her careful reserve.

She stopped. "What the fuck happened?" she asked. Her voice was deep, harsh, urgent, almost masculine; casting everything aside, every plan for being permissive to Targ. Had they slept together? She will always surprise me, Targ thought, she will always show me some new side. Targ put down her suitcase. He turned and began to walk back to the warehouse. He beckoned to her with a crooked finger.

"I don't want to play games, Targ. Not now."

He beckoned. Her heels clicked. He felt the tension and anger coming out of her; she wasn't absorbing any more. She followed. She wanted to ask a thousand questions. She possibly regretted she had broken the code of approving silence. When they got to the warehouse, Targ took her to the window and pointed in. She looked. Her hair, lank now, clumped into oily locks, shone like snakeskins against the grained gray wood and the dusty window gray; her nose was white against the dirt and her painted lips glittered along the window frame. "I don't see anything," she said.

"Do you see a sack?"

"What happened?"

"A white canvas sack?"

"All right. I see a white shape."

"Do you smell anything?"

Her nose crinkled; she sneezed as dust got into her nose. "Only the usual things."

Usual? "And they are . . . ?"

She sneezed again.

"Death's making you sneeze," Targ told her. "Look again." She did. "Do you see a white canvas sack tied with black ropes?"

"I think I do."

"That's our friend," Targ said and took her arm, turned her, and led her up the street.

"Was he killed?"

"He killed himself."

"You're a fool, Targ. You're a complete fool. Why didn't you stop it?"

"Stop it? How?"

"Why is he there?"

"They're sending him home. There's no room for him here. He doesn't fit into the usual categories."

"But like that? They've just flung him in there, like a sack of meal?"

"That's a cliché. Why, of all possible contents, is it a sack of meal?"

Targ could feel her looking at him, thinking, though not wanting to believe it—but having to accept its possibility—that he might have done it, might have killed the old man, or driven him to it. For sleeping with his wife. Yes. No. That was before. Before? "Obviously not," Targ told her. "Would I be free if I had? I'll admit he bored me almost to that point. I know; it's *my* fault." He waited for her to deny it. She didn't, but watched him. Harsh and cold face. Unremitting judgment.

"And of course I must, I *am* going to pay for it in some way. . . . Or perhaps I even paid in advance." Yes. That was it. He would tell the priest . . . no; the priest didn't count. It was only the officer who could force him to take the body off; tell *him*. "I know that. I haven't forgotten it for one instant, but I don't think I've come to *that* yet. He killed himself."

She didn't say anything. She took a deep breath, trying to control herself. Again. Began to calm herself, and her feelings of pity—always forgiving, even of fools—showed themselves as a flicker of grayish sunlight on her face, as a ruffle of her hair by a random moist breeze.

"No," he answered her. "I don't know why. Perhaps he had, as the priest has suggested, a spiritual crisis. Do you realize Targ doesn't know what that means?" And perhaps that was the message Kairos had been giving him; perhaps those were the words he had always misheard as pedantic chatter, always distorted by noise, mewls of sea gulls, the cheerful twitter of birds, the slap of a wave or the hiss of sickles as they sliced through the grain. He walked; she followed.

They passed the three-eyed woman standing there, looking quite ancient in the haze. Where had she come from? Targ bowed elaborately to her. She turned away and closed her eye so that only her third eye was open.

"What's going to happen now? Where are they burying him?"

"I said they were sending him home. Home is not a metaphor, not a euphemistic word."

They came to the pension. They walked upstairs. They passed the old man's room. The door was open. Targ pointed in. "He did it there. On the bed. That's where. Poison. I was next door at the time. Sleeping, or . . . I suppose one should be alert for these things all the time, shouldn't one?"

"You can't blame yourself for that, Targ."

She was retreating. He shouted, "You're goddamn right!"

"But you could have been more . . . sensitive."

"I'm a man who is trained to understand history. *History!* So how do you expect me to anticipate a statistical vagary? It simply is impossible. Who said I was blaming myself?"

They walked into Targ's room. He put down her suitcase. *"Ecco!"* he said. "Home. When are your friends coming?"

"They said they'd be back by morning."

"Good. We'll be able to get away."

"Get away?"

"There'll be no burial. They decide, the authorities, that I'm to be responsible for the body."

"But why won't they bury the body?"

"There are many reasons, none of which are clear to me. The priest won't bury a suicide . . . evil, you see. The officer decries the introduction of the lack of order, and how his paper work will be set askew. . . . You remember how the compulsion of paper work infects us all. There is no institutionalized ground."

"Well, *we* could bury him."

"No. You don't understand. Not here."

"Why not?"

"Why not? You know how it is with primitives. The islanders chatter at the ghost. Desecration of the sacred soil. Something to do with upsetting climatic cycles. Antifertility . . . antifertilizer . . . poisoning-the-well stuff. The harvest may be ruined. . . . It's classic superstition."

"But . . ."

"So I'm responsible and no one's offended. Solomon's wisdom rises out of the unresolvable jurisdictional disputes."

"But we hardly know Mr. Kairos."

"I told them all this."

"And what are we supposed to do with . . . with Mr. Kairos?"

"Presumably deliver him to the mainland, where they will know how to handle these things."

"That's not too unreasonable."

"You're turning stupid. We will be stuck with it; you'll see. We will have to cart this thing here and there. We will have to go all over the world, back home, prop it up in the living room. Our own personal sarcophagus. Better than slides. Do you suppose your new friends would . . . but no, you did say that only we were invited." Targ laughed. "Oh, I had some wild thoughts about burials at sea. On the other hand, it would round out their scene, wouldn't it? We could take Kairos abroad disguised as a package . . . an antiquity; even sell him . . . maybe even come back, land at night, and bury him. No. They'd never let us take him away in any but the prescribed manner."

She didn't say anything and for once Targ couldn't read what she was thinking.

"We should take him back."

"To where?"

"His home."

"Where's that?"

"To where we found him. To where he was staying. We must take him back."

"He really wanted to be here. If I could describe for you his love of this place . . . It will spoil our cruise with your new friends. No. This could solve all our difficulties. We just go. Let *them* make him a part of this earth . . . or ship him; do whatever they want to do," Targ said.

"We can't do that."

"We will. Just depart early in the morning."

"We have to take him . . ."

"Him? There is no 'him.' "

". . . and then we can return at night and bury him."

"Your friends might not like all this tacking around."

"I can always get the film makers to persuade the owner."

"Are you getting sentimental? *It.* No."

She stopped arguing. She knew better. Now he would have to watch her.

Then Targ took Helen outside and showed her around the island while telling her all about it. He showed her the reapers; the men, the women, and now even the children working, all in their mad race through the haze, trying to gather it all in before the wet winds spoiled it. Targ showed her the temple. Targ walked her along the beach and showed her the strange artificial chasm.

She appeared bored. The more bored she was, the more he embellished and emphasized the place's special charm. He quoted Mr. Kairos. He described how, as a young, romantic man, Kairos had come to this island for the first time. He became a little strident, repeating things, making the same kinds of mistakes he used to make as a young teacher, substituting stress and repetition for explanation, as if it should all be as self-evident as an axiom. Trag began to tell her of the nature of Mr. Kairos's love for this island.

He noticed it had not gotten any hazier. Perhaps the islanders would bring it off.

They stood on the beach for a while and waited for strange sounds to be gathered and materialize, but nothing happened. He contemplated having sex with her . . . perhaps as a way of getting her out of her boredom, of impressing the lesson in her. It was too hot and sandy here. They left. They came back to the town. It was almost dark. They went into the café. There was no one to serve them, even though they waited for a long time. They were all out in the fields, watching the sky, hoping, praying, or cursing, Targ supposed. He banged on the table. He went into the back room. No one was there.

The officer came in to check on Targ. He bowed graciously to Helen. It was a remembered gesture, vaguely continental, urbane, but unnatural to him, as if he had learned it from the movies. He preened himself and tried to act out his version of something called sophistication. Targ invited him to sit.

"We can't get anything to eat," he complained. "You see, of course, that my wife is here."

The officer shrugged his shoulders. "There is nothing I can do now."

"Is this the way to treat a lady?"

"I regret . . ." the officer regretted and he deplored and he bent closer to them, conspiratorially, though there was no one else in the room. He intimated that but for the dogmatism, the superstitious dogmatism of the priest, the intransigent superstition of the islanders, it would all have been a simple matter, and so much more civilized. And he regretted, further, another delay. Targ and Helen must wait a day longer than usual because the ferry sailors, being natives, had to help with the harvest before the winds came.

Helen's lips were compressed and tight. Targ squeezed her hand. She didn't say anything about her new friend's boat.

"I saw the body today."

The officer looked at Targ with raised eyebrows.

"Did you just throw it into the warehouse or did you carefully prop it up in that ludicrous position?" Targ asked. The pressure of her hand warned him, but he said, "Because it was most amusing."

"You said yourself, my friend, that he is just meat," the officer said. He stood up, tugged at his straps, and readjusted his cap. "I regret the inconvenience, madame."

"But he's a human being," Helen said.

"Yet, but as your husband has pointed out, he is no longer that, is he? Does it matter to him?" He spoke the words lovingly. "If a body is undignified in its aspect, if he has died in an undignified manner, that is to say a lawless manner, it is the same thing. At any rate, it doesn't matter. I don't see why it upsets you," he told Targ.

"It's not that so much. . . . As the priest said, he was a proud man."

"Priests always talk like that," the officer said. "It makes one lose one's view of essentials to speak of pride. He was messy. He was lawless. He was criminal. He upset things. He left loose ends. He was willful and inconsiderate. Ultimately he may have put all our lives in danger; even more, endangered our position here. You see, out there the fleets contend . . . waiting, under the guise of maneuvers . . . perhaps even wanting the islanders to rise up. The question of agricultural assistance . . . bases . . . And one must say this about my friend the priest: as long as they remain superstitious, there is always the possibility of conversion. It is easy to convert from religion to religion, but not from atheism to religion. The Church has put more than thirteen hundred years into this place. My own government . . ."

"But that's ridiculous."

"Is it? And he was, do you deny, and *you* are, do you deny, American?"

"A person in despair has no nationality."

"How stupid do you think I am? Not everyone gets to go to the Fouché Academy. No nationality? You see, one can tell a lot about the personality from national origins. In the larger, in the developed world, there is room for such acts to be discounted, but here there is not."

"So you're pretending not to notice this act by shipping the body back?"

"It is *because* I notice this act that I dare not set administrative precedents," the officer said. He saluted Helen, turned, and went quickly out.

After a while Targ remembered that they had had nothing to eat or drink and he went out to try and find the officer, but couldn't. They went back to the pension.

There was only a single bed in each room. Helen slept in Targ's bed and he went and slept in the other room.

Why had her mind been changed so quickly?

12

But she came in the night when he was almost asleep. Her timing was perfect; her sense of camouflage superb. Targ perceived her dim figure there, standing in the darkness, darker than the faint light from the window that streamed in over the shoulders of the hanging suit. "But the man died here," Targ said. She said nothing. "In this bed." She leaned down, kissed Targ, pushed him a little to the side, and lay down beside him. "You are the resurrection and the life, maybe?" he said in pure Tragese. It was supposed to be years now since he had enjoyed her, or even wanted to, but making love *here* excited him.

"He should be buried."

"Yes, he should," he said between her breasts.

"I'm not joking. I'm very upset. We have to bury him."

"Full honors," he told her pubic hairs. And they began to make love.

But that seemed to go on without relief for too long a time and, though the body kept responding, Targ felt no ultimate pleasure. Every time he was about to ejaculate, he was reminded of Kairos and the sense of urgency and panic, the sense of something having to be done or something not having to be done, of having to . . . he didn't know what, returned. And it fretted at him in the darkness.

"Please . . ." the mouth of her vagina broadcast into the microphone of his penis.

The voice traffic became very heavy again and now they also heard the babble of military commands in many machine-scrambled languages. It was as if they were fucking among thousands. He stifled his voice, but she did not, almost as if her excitement was being amplified by the voices. She had always been an of-the-group person anyway. It seemed to him as if she was not-doing something, he didn't know what, to prevent him from orgasming. . . . Till he agreed? Finally he was too tired to continue though the excitement was still in him, sustained but momentarily dormant, and his penis would not detumesce. Outside, the wind was rising, rising. He lay still, half asleep. She squirmed under him; his weight was getting to be too much for her.

But then she turned him around and rode him like a colossa.

Someone had come in and was standing, almost absorbed by the darkness, and watching them. The one who watched, or the watching, excited him. He began to get his second wind. Helen's face, framed by her hanging hair, instead of being distorted by her intensity, her passionate concentration, in the usual way, looked almost abstracted, studious. He smiled. He knew what she did not. Why did the other one in the darkness wait? For what?

They came closer and closer to orgasm. The figure in shadows moved. It was the woman with three eyes. She came close to their bodies and stood there, as if listening intently, waiting for the right pitch of chorused screamyell. She reared back a little; her hands clawed; she swooped. Her hands taloned Helen's buttocks and pulled. Helen screamed and writhed in pain. He was almost at the point of complete explosion. Helen's vagina clamped. He felt pulled up with Helen. Helen tried to turn and flail behind her without interrupting her motions, but she came loose with an enormous sucking pop. His body continued its motion, half launched into the air. A claw grasped his penis and squeezed, squeezed. His ejaculation was ricocheted back and exploded inside him; warmth flowed from some center, suffusing his body.

Helen was on the floor, writhing. The woman with three eyes was gone. He collapsed and lay still.

After a long time he could hear Helen stirring, turning, the floor creaking under her. He turned his head; he didn't have the strength for more. He watched her begin to get up. She began by pushing her legs under her body, which elevated her behind; her breasts trailed on the floor. Then she got up on her elbows, but her face was still on the floor. She raised herself slowly, trying to straighten her arms, but they trembled too much and she fell back onto her elbows and stayed there for a long while. He couldn't have moved to help her, even if he'd wanted to. The wind had died down. It was still humid. Helen's wet body glistened. And then she heaved herself up, reeled, caught herself, and went into the darkness again. Targ fell asleep.

Targ woke, feeling very alert, healthy, as though he had recovered from a long illness. The feeling of well-being gave way to a terrible hunger. The need for food bent him over so that he sat with his chest against his knees for a long time; his back was bowed and his head fell, almost touching his shins. His arms hung limply, the palms of his hands on the tops of his feet. Each hunger spasm held Targ rigid for a second in his position, and then shook him again as though something were being squeezed out of him rhythmically. He began to sweat while the contractions went on. Soon his body was wet. His face was wet. He could feel the sweat dripping down his face, through the rough stubble on his chin, dripping onto his knees; little rills of perspiration continued on down his shins or back down his thighs, where the drops joined the humid moisture around his groin. The stupidity and discomfort of it kept annoying Targ; the rustle of the suit sleeves reminded him. Keep calm, Targ thought, only till morning. Right after the islanders had gone to the fields to harvest, when Helen's friend's yacht came to take them away, he would have time to get away and leave them to do with the body what they wanted: ship it or bury it. It would be a matter of getting on the boat unseen.

No. He couldn't do that. He would dispose of the body. He must have known what he would have to do all the time. But he still did not accept it; he began to move as if movement, the doing of ordinary things, would disguise what he would do, till some moment of crisis and commitment came, and then he would quickly betray himself. Trag got up and went over to the window and looked, pushing the suit roughly aside. The hanger on which it hung slipped to the side. The suit fell down, brushing Trag's body as it fell. The hunger pangs went away; the terrible need was gone. And Trag began to feel better, stronger. The restlessness persisted and Targ thought again that he must only wait awhile and it would be over, only wait and he would escape, and surely they couldn't follow him over the water. He rehearsed it, acting it out over and over, making the necessary moves in his mind as if watching himself. But Trag could not be calm; he could not sleep. He had to get up again and get dressed because the hunger came again, made him rise and move to escape. There was a rhythm to it; he should time the waves and prepare for them.

Trag went downstairs. He stood for a moment outside. There was no one in the streets at all. He could smell the sea more clearly now. The walls of the buildings were faintly luminous planes. Trag walked swiftly through blackness among the disembodied planes, going in the direction of the wharf. The sound of the nearness of the waves and the sudden zone of sea smell; the feel of ground beneath his feet (no longer hard dirt and street stone) gave way to slight creak and sway; he was on the wharf. What if his cues were wrong? Did he smell something suddenly, smell it more clearly than the heavy salt smell of the sea? The body? Surely the smell of its dissolution couldn't come through the canvas sack, move along the air, through the warehouse walls, along the wharf, persist in the damp breeze to reach him? Targ thought of the sack, the precarious position, the black ropes, and wondered if it had fallen to the floor yet. Perhaps the imbalance propagated the waves of smell? Targ retched.

He stopped by the warehouse and tried to look in. He could see nothing at all. He felt for the lock and wondered what he would do if he found it. Would he lean down and listen to the tumblers clicking, indicating the combination of the lock? And what would he do if he *could* open it? Targ touched the lock. The brass was coated with moisture; wet, cold, greasy. Feeling the power to tear the latch loose from the rotted, eroded door and jamb, Trag wrenched it suddenly, pulling strongly in spite of his weakness. Latch and lock came away. But what would he *really* do if he got inside? Straighten out the body, lay it down, let it rest . . . or move it to some higher place and let it rest there, off the floor? Silly. Dead is dead, thought Targ. Call it sin, illegality, or disorderliness, it was stiff and stinking flesh. Leave it at that. Move out in the morning. Escape. Forget it all. Yet it might be amusing, Targ thought, if he took the body out, brought it somewhere else—the café, for instance—and propped it up in one of the chairs. He giggled. Leave a note. "You were running out of meat, so . . ." He looked around to see if anyone had heard.

Trag dropped the lock on the floor and swung the door open.

He stood in darkness more total than he had known before. Was he afflicted with night blindness? Why didn't he drink carrot juice instead of hard liquor? Go back. Go back. What was Trag trying to do? But it was merely darkness, no more, and not the gray emptiness which lay behind all blackness; that was comforting. Trag stepped inside. The door closed slowly behind him, perhaps slowly blown shut by the wind. Targ sniffed at the darkness, trying to find the old man's body by its smell. He could only smell the mustiness of the long-disused shed, the smell of something wet seeping up from the water underneath, the faint effluvia of rotted fish. Trag took tentative steps. He heard a great rumbling somewhere. It was coming from his stomach. He stopped to wait, but no cramp waves followed. Trag kept walking slowly into the darkness, testing each step, feeling his heels sink into the spongy wood of the floor as he moved toward where he was sure he had seen the body.

Trag felt something just as his toe settled itself down in its swing, bringing him to the end of a stride. He bent and felt the roughness of the canvas under his hands. The something inside it was hard, stiffened like an assemblage of sticks. Trag found, by feeling, that it was a torso, stick legs, stiffened arms, a head held in a permanent loll. Therefore it was Kairos. Trag wondered if the bastards had bothered to shut Kairos's eyes. He could feel what it would feel like to have the old man's open eyes brushed by the canvas. He shuddered. The sack was tied tightly with tarred ropes. Little sticky pieces came off in his hands. Trag tried not to inhale; he might breathe in the stench of rotting body and be sick. But there was no smell. Trag bent, heaved, and tried to lay it down flat on the floor. It toppled, but he could not straighten it so that it would lie stretched out. It remained askew; rigid pieces of sack kept sticking up into the air. No matter which way Trag turned it, it wouldn't lie flat. A monstrous upended crab, unresting and distorted, was in the sack. Trag tried to force parts of it flat, leaning on it, but the strength of the limbs in their frozen position was too strong for him. He was afraid he might break off a piece. Targ stood up. He thought: go away, forget it, leave. He couldn't. That dead Mr. Kairos, gnarled and thus undignified in the sack, seemed uncomfortable, those unclosed eyes irritated and bothersome. The thought of Kairos taken out of the sack and put into the café was too rich. But would he fit into a chair this way?

Trag grasped the sack and tried to swing it up over his shoulder. If he went outside he might see what he was doing. But he wasn't sure, unable to see, what was the best way to place the body on his shoulder. The body was too rigid, hard to handle, and kept slipping lower on his shoulder. He had to keep knee-bending and heaving the weight upward to bounce it into a more secure position. It remained unbalanced, refusing to settle, thrusting out in different directions, teetering precariously as he walked with it. He was half dizzy with hunger now, half choked with trying not to breathe, even though there was nothing unpleasant coming from the sack. Had the body been miraculously preserved? How long would it be before it started to decompose? He became afraid the body would liquefy suddenly, while he had it on his shoulder, its fluid weight dropping to both ends of the sack, beginning to seep through the sacking, drenching him with decomposition.

Trag reeled under the weight of it, even though it was, thank God, surprisingly light. Old men didn't weigh much, Trag thought, and Kairos had been thin. He tried to move forward. He turned around in place a few times, building up momentum, and then, translating that circular movement to linearity, lurched and started. He could hear the creaking of the floorboards and it seemed, for a second, as though he would sink through them. The rotten and crackling wood would give, dumping Trag and Kairos into the water under the wharf. And would he, in the water and barely able to swim, be able to find his way out from among the pilings? There was something amusing about the idea. His stomach rumbled. He belched. His breath, as he tasted it rising past his mouth, was worse, much worse, than the body could ever smell.

Trag managed to find the door. He used whatever part of Mr. Kairos that projected ahead of him, feet or head—he couldn't be sure which—to push open the door. On the wharf, Trag could faintly see the sea, a gray sheet stretching away on three sides of the black rectangle that was the wharf. Behind was the black, more solid mass of the island, which swallowed building and Trag and fused all into one. He started in that direction.

But when he came to the café, he realized how silly, how childish it would be to leave the body there . . . as silly as throwing it in a heap into a dusty corner: a piece of Targ's humorous magic. Kairos deserved more than that. He kept going. He walked through the town, trying to step quietly on the stones and hard dirt. He kept going, past the police station, past the church, and left the town. He walked uphill slowly, stopping now and then to heave the weight of the body up, moving his shoulder slightly to catch it in a more comfortable position. Perhaps it was best of all simply to bury Kairos and leave quietly and forget about it all. Or should he go to the top of the island and leave the body in the temple? He thought about how the officer would look, and how the priest would throw up his hands, and how the islanders would behave after he and Helen were gone in the morning, when they finally discovered the body was missing. What would they substitute for it? For there had to be a token that all processes begun had been finished; that evil, or disruption, had been cast out. Trag began to laugh a little. "Well, old man," Trag told the sack, "you've caused enough trouble but at least you'll be able to spend your time here, though God knows why you should want that. And just think, they'll harvest grain, or pick off olives, or goats will eat something or other containing your recomposed substance. And then you'll come out as shit and go back into the earth. You'll belong. Not in the way you wanted, but you'll belong. Consoled?" And he laughed again.

But when Trag had got about halfway up the hill, he found he had left the road. He wandered around, trying to get back on it. The stalk prickles stabbed at him and he was sure that, after a while, the points had penetrated his socks, shredding them; his ankles were scratched and bleeding. And soon he was tired, going downhill because it was easier, stumbling a little, trying to catch himself and turn because the way should be upward. But the body had a tendency to overbalance and he had to make short rushes to maintain balance. He said, "Easy. Don't fall. Don't be afraid. Stop moving around."

After a while the ground leveled out and he was walking through sand, feeling the grains crumple and hiss under his feet. Trying to turn back and go up the hill, Trag felt something wet, cooling his scratches . . . the sea surging around his ankles. He turned again but found himself going deeper and deeper into it, wetting himself to his knees. He turned and turned but kept going deeper. He thought, calmly enough, that he must not panic. Did corpses sink, Trag wondered, or would Kairos, because he felt as light as a balsa life preserver, really float? Would he be able to keep afloat holding on to Kairos? Or, if they fell in and Trag let go, Kairos would have his sea burial after all. No, that was a compromise. In any case, they were too close to shore. The body would be cast up very soon. The comedy would start again. He stood and felt the strong though still soft tug of waters and wondered if the tide was running out or coming in; should he follow it? High above, too high and too faint to give enough light, the silver of moon's radiance was scraped away by the haze that passed below. Trag thought he should really leave Kairos here. All he had to do was let go and be gone in the morning. The beams of strong naval searchlights broke up into a universal golden radiance. And yet —he didn't know how he had come to it—he was determined now to bury the body.

And for one second he could see where the island lay. The water must have been very shallow here, the land sinking gradually, because he had got very far out. It almost seemed (even though distances at night, and especially in moonlight and searchlight, were deceptive) as if he were a mile or more away from the land. He was stuck in the middle of something shimmering and molten, a vast plain of fire relieved only by the solid shape of the island with that temple, which was caught for one second, white and brilliant, as enticing as it had appeared in the center of the brochure. "See," Trag said. "See, it's another lie." And he turned and began to make his way back to the island. **Beside him, a woman's mature contralto voice, languorous in spite of the German she spoke, said, "The moonlight, Rinaldo, how beautiful it is."**

"It's only the dead and reflective face of a burned-out body. Already they've defiled it," a young, tenor, and dramatically

bitter voice replied. "The beauty's elsewhere."

"Rinaldo, kiss me. Kiss me there where three children have been born. Let my lips be midwife to another kind of child." And there was a little silence, and the contralto rose into a grand operatic aria and fell slowly, tragically, into sobs and silence. And the young voice said, "But, to be sure, it has its merits, for the goddesses have stolen and saved the moon's magic."

"Don't weaken," Trag called, but they didn't seem to hear him at all.

Before Trag reached the island, the moonlight was hazed out again and he was in darkness, though he knew he was on the way back. But suddenly he plunged into a slough which seemed to go down and down. Trag thought he must have turned seaward accidentally, the weight steering him wrong. And the waters were now drawing him away and out to sea. Let go. The canvas began to soak and become heavy. Drop him, go back, drop him now, Targ thought. And when the water reached his chin, he had to fight to assure himself he was on the way back to the island. The waters began to recede. And then he was on dry land, walking through the sand, walking up the hill, walking through uncut grain which beat at his legs in waves, his feet sticking in the muck of the soft soil, bearing the body. Trag didn't know how long he had climbed but he kept going. "Soon," he kept muttering. "Soon. We'll be there soon."

He ran into someone. The light was turning nacreous. The imbalance of the body tending downward, an unevenness of the ground, the light collision into someone, the tiredness, made him fall. Trag felt something wrenching in his shoulder; his ankle twisted; his face smashed against something hard, like a fist, or a bone. He was sure, though it might have been another effusion of perspiration, he had begun to bleed from his nose. He blacked out for a while.

When he opened his eyes, he was lying in the grain and looking up. The body of old Kairos was lying on his belly. Trag saw the steady grayness of the morning sky, almost black with clouds. Thick legs stood all around and over him, looking distorted from his position so that he felt surrounded by giants. They all held sickles. The points hung downward. Their faces were impassive, kept that way by rage, discipline, or by the fact that they were unused to expressing emotion . . . or he had no way of reading the emotion. Trag said, "I have delivered a new hand to help with the harvesting. Help me up." No one moved. They shrunk back a little from him and he saw that they were afraid of him or what he had. Trag leaned his head back and let the stalks of grain crisscross his sight of them, almost as if to shut them out. He closed his eyes as if to nap awhile.

He was jabbed. Trag opened his eyes. They were still standing around him, but a little closer. No one said anything. Their faces hadn't changed, but Trag believed that something had taken place behind their implacable brown looks. One of them leaned down and pricked Trag again in the side and gestured at him to stand up. Trag tried to rise but the weight was too heavy and he couldn't. He told them, making gestures, to lift the sack so he could sit up. They drew back a little. Trag faintly heard the drumbeat start for the reaping to begin. The furious voices of the leaders began to shout at them. One of them turned away and waved—Trag couldn't be sure in what direction—summoning. Trag tried to rise again, but he fainted.

13

Targ was in some dim grayness and thought that at last what he had feared had finally happened. He had gone mad; or the world had burned down and it was all ashes. Targ was in a gray nothingness from which nothing could extract him, from which Helen could never call him back, from which he couldn't run away this time. And if he lived in this world, if he screamed from this *here,* could they hear him?

But Trag remembered. Piece by piece it dimly reconstructed itself. The officer had been there; the priest had made some placating signs of exorcism over Trag and had mumbled over the trampled grain.

And they, the officer and the priest, had to carry Trag and Kairos down because no one else would touch them. They had lifted him. Kairos still lay across his body. Using Trag as a litter, they carried them down that way, sweating and grunting and cursing and arguing all the way, united at last. Trag remembered. There had been a temple and a woman with three eyes and a fly fluttering at an eye and Helen had met them at the entrance to the village and he had said, "Lo, how I ride in triumph through Persepolis . . ." and he remembered nothing after that. So Trag decided he had just gone mad to escape the silliness of the whole thing. But now he was lying on a floor. What had they done with Mr. Kairos? "Where are you?" Trag asked and saw that the sack was lying next to him. "You old fool; you gave it away. I tried," Trag told the tar-roped sack.

There was a lamp now, at one end, barely visible, hanging from a chain, flickering in wind that came through a hole or opening he couldn't see. As his eyes became used to the grayness, he saw that he was not mad after all, but they had merely put him, as well as his old friend, in the warehouse for safekeeping. Trag stood up. The floorboards were spaced about half an inch apart. Trag saw the water moiling underneath his feet. Above him, suspended from the beams, were ropes and a chain hoist and above that the roof met in a pointed groin where it seemed to be smokier but lighter. Birds flew in and out of that space. They came out of the grayness, flickered briefly, fluttering wildly, and flew on into the grayness again. There were piles of burlap sacking around him; probably for the harvest. As his eyes got used to the dimness, he could see that the sides were not lined with shadow or planes or abstract solids but with pieces of sculpture: statuary, shattered plinths, pedestals, chunks of frieze, disembodied arms, half heads, jaw-mouths, pieces of nose, breasts of marble and phalluses of obsidian, portions of neck. There was one huge chunk of jaw, about six feet high, in which the mouth was open. The artistry was so fine, Roman, and careful that the neck muscles and neck veins were defined to the point of almost throbbing in marble, while the mouth seemed to scream eternally. The roped sack had been tumbled down and was lying in a position bodies couldn't assume.

There were labels attached to the statuary. That solved the mystery of the missing antiques: they were being stolen for sale to the museums and grand universities of the world. "The laugh is on you, Mr. Kairos. It was pointless to come here after all. All you had to do was wait and it would have come to you." He picked up a label and looked at it. It came *from* America, Connecticut to New York, New York to its first destination, *here,* Terminus, and then it would go back to the Zaharoff Collection. Other labels showed that the sculpture was all routed through here to famous collections. Fakes? It didn't matter . . . the *arrangement* was.

Outside, the wind was rising, rattling and creaking the warehouse.

He remembered, suddenly, a vase-lamp his mother had had in their house. Blue, too-blue shiny cheap porcelain, stamped out in the thousands, with a painted classical motif, figures acting out fragments of legends, Poseidons and Zeuses and nymphs and mermaids. Italian. Dreadful. Cheap. Trag had grown to hate it more each time he came home from college. She couldn't understand his hatred. His hatred had been wrong; misdirected. He saw that clearly now. That vase, connected to an elaborate gold-filigreed base, Moorish, should have been here too. It belonged here, somewhere in this sequence. If he could place that lamp here in its proper place . . . He laughed to think what it would do to the museums of the world.

Rattling and creaking, the warehouse was rising the wind outside.

Trag was dizzy. The room circled quickly around him a few times. Yes. Of that he was sure. Targ kept telling himself that everything was all right. It was the day the yacht would be coming in and they would get away. The room stopped. He remembered. He had been brought here with Mr. Kairos and locked up. Therefore he would have to wait until the ferry began running again. He would have to go with the body after all . . . with that stinking corpse (they would wait that long, deliberately). Trag raged because they had no care or consideration for what they did with the cold meat. Trag moved away from the body, but tried to look as if he were merely shifting his position, so as not to offend Mr. Kairos. But he had to look, even if apologetically, at the distorted shape beneath the sack. He thought: Friend, how can you possibly be comfortable in that position? It makes *me* restless. The body didn't smell. Of that he was sure now. He decided that the sacking held the stench in. How long would it be before the smell escaped?

Trag got up and went to the window. Everything was gray, crusted through the crusted glass, moist and overhanging. Low clouds were about to shear off the top of the island. Someone stood at the other side of the wharf, leaning against some of the pilings, watching the warehouse. He looked carefully. He rubbed a half-clear space on the glass. It was the three-eyed woman. He yelled at her. She didn't answer. There was nothing to do but wait it out. Trag went back and sat down beside the sack. He couldn't sit there long. He had to watch.

After a while the officer and Helen came by. She was carrying her suitcase. Trag could see them walking past the window. She didn't look in the direction of the warehouse. The yacht had come, Trag thought, and she would leave him. It was over. But after a while they returned. The officer unlocked the door and they entered. Helen didn't say anything. Her face was set, hard.

"I'm not mad," Trag told her.

"You are, Targ; you've spoiled everything," she said.

"Targ? Targ? Who is Targ? I know who you are."

The officer told Trag how foolish, how unrealistic he had been about the whole thing, how shockingly romantic the whole venture had been. At first, he said, Trag's attitude of indifference, an indifference of pure reason almost, had pleased him. But he had disappointed the officer by a regression to superstition worse than the priest's, worse, much worse, than the islanders'. Their position on the island was precarious. They were the only link to the world, the only hope for these savages. Trag had, by his silly, intransigent, whimsical attitudes, placed them all in danger. At first the natives had felt that the coming of the winds was due to the presence of the unlucky Kairos alone. Then they said the problem was Trag. Now they *all* were associated with the body. To be frank, the officer said, it was with great difficulty that they had extricated themselves from that position. For Trag they could do nothing but hope he stayed alive.

"But we live in modern times," Trag said.

"Some of us do; others do not," the officer said. He told Trag that he had done the worst thing: to bring that unlucky body into contact with their soil, which had defiled the harvest, undone the efficacy of prayer and administration. And of course, not only did Trag have bad luck but he was a malicious carrier of it. "It is a primitive notion of disease carried too far . . . but one that can lead to death."

Helen didn't say anything.

"It could all have been smoothed over," the officer concluded, "if you had let it."

"But look at what you've done," Trag said, waving at the contorted shape beneath the canvas, tied into that ludicrous position by the ropes; including, in that wave, the statuary. And as Trag said it, he could feel the stupidity of what he said now, and couldn't help being angry.

The officer told them that this was neither here nor there, that it was all regrettable, but he washed his hands of it all. In what way did espousing the cause of a dead man, a stupid, willful, and disorderly one, trying to bury the man, alter things?

At any rate, they could only hope that nothing happened, that everything went all right, that the rain didn't come before the harvest was in. Because, the officer said, if all failed, who knew what they might do to them, the body and Trag? He told Trag that Helen had refused to leave with the pleasure boat. Trag had a fine wife, did he understand that?

"Why didn't you go?" he asked Helen.

She didn't answer.

When the ferry began to run again, Trag and his wife must take the body and leave, the officer said. Other than wait, he could do nothing, for the warehouse was watched; nothing to do but wait and possibly pray, he added ironically.

Trag insisted they couldn't leave the body like that. Helen turned away; the officer didn't even seem to hear. They left.

Trag looked out the window, which was framed by two massive marble shapes. She with three eyes, she watched the warehouse. Trag turned around and looked at the sack.

Now Targ imagined that the stench escaped its containment, rose till it filled the great room, slinking into every corner, clinging to the great cool, sweating marble shapes, permeating the musty cracks, rising higher and higher still, Targ was sure, till it was up among the rafters and the crossbeams and in the groin and flowing along the ropes and chains, driving the birds away. "No!" Targ screamed and began to take burlap sacking to throw it over the canvas. He worked furiously till there was a great mound obscuring it, a mound much higher than Targ.

After a while the dust from the burlap settled, but the smell kept coming through after all. Targ retched, but there was nothing to throw up. His dry spasms shook Targ; he heard the dry clicks of his throat, each one of which caused him to recoil, driving him back a little. Finally he stopped retching. He felt weak again.

He had buried nothing. He could smell it. He could *see* the distorted shape, a shape that had to be straightened out into the semblance of a man, through the weight of burlap. Not a thousand pounds of sacking could make him feel sure that the body was straightened out and resting comfortably, Targ thought. Targ was afraid.

But Trag began to remove the sacking. He heard a muffled shout behind him. He turned. The view from the window was blocked by a head. A voice shouted furiously at Trag. Trag half turned and raised his hand, his thumb pushed between his first and second fingers, his other hand over the crook in his elbow; he elevated the forearm and hand mockingly. The voice shouted furiously again. The squatness of the shape showed it could only be the woman with three eyes. He repeated the obscene gesture, yelling, "Fuck your soul." After a while the head was gone. Trag turned and continued to remove the sacking. After it was all off, he prepared to bend down and untie the ropes.

He began to laugh. He went over to one of the statues, took off the label, and brought it over to attach to his old good great friend Mr. Kairos. Yes, he would bury Mr. Kairos in the temple after all. But when they came to get Mr. Kairos out of the temple, he would be decomposed and could never be restored and extracted. . . . It would break the chain.

The rope knots were almost fused; black, recalcitrant, sticky. Pieces of tarred strand came loose. Trag's fingers became abraded. Little tarry scratches began to bleed. Prayer. Yes, prayer. Of course, he knew nothing of prayer; of course, he knew the prayers of thousands of societies. Who remembered the *feel* of what one has discarded for so long a time and relegated to the warehouse of childhood remnants? Not Targ; Trag did.

And yet he must, must go through with it. Remembering nothing, none of the old inadequate words, the dead gestures, because everything had been shaken loose and was all mixed up in his head, Trag walked around Kairos, bobbing his head, kneeling swiftly from moment to moment, standing, throwing out his arms, folding his hands, making patting, comforting gestures to the air over Kairos, wailing, keening. And hearing the wail echoes reverberate and reflect and come back at him brought tears to his eyes and fresh memories of Kairos. And he bent, again and again, trying to work the ropes loose.

Certainly he said, "Dust thou art and to dust shall ye return." Everyone remembered that one and he said it to signify many things. Yet Trag remembered—and the thought made him hilarious—that dust Kairos had not been, and there would have to be a refining process; one he would certainly have to oversee. Putrefaction, liquefaction, purification; and drying out and finally petrifaction. And then, like stone disassembled finally into its constituent, component, constructional parts, rock bottom that is particles, he would finally have to be preserved and emplaced on this island, on one of the very spots from which monuments were removed and replaced from the store in the warehouse, and so made a monument.

Every now and then Trag would stand to rest and straighten out his bent back. He tried to rub the tar and blood off his hands. He checked to see if he could slip some of the loops off, but without disturbing the body. He found he had got quite used to the smell of it; it was even pleasant. Below him, seen down between the boards, the waters were roiled into white-tipped wavelets that beat the pilings.

"Putrefaction to petrifaction," Trag said and laughed. There would be a long time before Kairos passed through those stages of dis-development. How could he speed it up? Yes, get him upright and place him among the monuments and pieces of monuments. Were they arranged in historical sequence? Where would he place Kairos to discontinue the sequence, break it up? How could he speed up the process of dissolution? Eat him and shit him out quickly? He tried to stop himself and think through what he was doing, but there was no time left and so he kept on working. But he found he now remembered everything again, everything he had forgotten in front of his classes, but not in the same way. A piece of rope came loose. And then a few other pieces. The strands dissolved into strings and threads and into mere tar. Trag began stuffing the pieces carefully between the boards, dropping them into the water below, watching them dissolve and sink from sight forever.

Trag heard murmurs outside. And then another shout. And then the beginning of a roar. And then the sound a cyclone makes, hundreds of railroad trains. The chill, damp winds came forcefully through the cracks now; the wind wailed. Trag heard their angry and stupid cry above the wind. The canvas was almost loose. Trag got up and went to a window. He saw them pouring down the street. Helen stepped out of a side street and for one second, the wind blowing her jacket back like wings, tried to stand in their way. Her body was hit, lifted, whirled above their heads, her long arms and legs flailing, fluttering over them, dropping in among them, and pieces were then spewed up and out.

Emerging from their midst to run in front of them, or chased by them, were the officer and the priest, side by side, each trying to shove the other out of the way and assume leadership, bouncing together and then apart. The crowd caught up to them, pushed them; and they ran ahead faster, still trying to jostle one another aside. The mob came on. They carried sickles. Their wet faces and wet bodies were already dimmed by the thick flow of wet and cloud-bearing wind. The officer and the priest were engulfed and spewed up and out. Trag turned away. "I haven't forgotten you," he told Mr. Kairos. He bent down over the canvas. His back shivered and twitched and trembled.

They crashed the door open. The heavy air, which held the perpetual island stink of droppings, came sweeping in, flowing in from all over the island.

They were all shouting at Trag. They had forgotten, or did not use, the mainland language, roaring in something guttural, primitive, plosive, half human, the words coming in gouts.

They were gone now, Helen, the officer, and the priest. He could stop now.

But Trag undid the canvas carefully, lovingly. The lamp swung in the wind slowly, in long arcs, scattering sparks of light back and forth.

The islanders had stopped. He waited for them.

He turned his back to them. The body's smell rose up fully now, rich, sweet, pleasant, like hot confectioner's sugar. Hands grasping, arms embracing, fingers clutching, legs clasping, mouth open to bite, he threw himself on Kairos.

The floor of the warehouse vibrated as they came up behind Trag.

PS3575 U75 I8
+An island death +Yurick, Sol, 192
0 00 02 0211262 9
MIDDLEBURY COLLEGE